Miss
Oriented
AND THE BILLIONAIRE

Other Books By Lorin Grace

American Homespun Series
Waking Lucy
Remembering Anna
Reforming Elizabeth
Healing Sarah

Artists & Billionaires
Mending Fences
Mending Christmas
Mending Walls
Mending Images
Mending Words
Mending Hearts

Hastings Security
Not the Bodyguard's Baby
Not the Bodyguard's Widow
Not the Bodyguard's Boss
Not the Bodyguard's Princess
Not the Bodyguard's Bride

Misadventures in Love
Miss Guided

AND THE BILLIONAIRE

LORIN GRACE

CURRANT
CREEK PRESS

Cover Design © 2019 LJP Creative
Photos © iStock; aphotostory

Formatting by LJP Creative
Edits by Eschler Editing

Published by Currant Creek Press
North Logan, Utah

First edition: July 2019
ISBN: 978-1-970148-04-6

Katelyn
LOVE YOU FOREVER.

Misadventures in Love

In response to the requests of several of our alumni, "virtual crowns" suitable for posting on social media will now be awarded. Thank you to our very own Miss Guided, Gina Swann Batiste, for donating her skills in designing them. Current and past crown holders will receive their e-crowns via email. Please make sure you keep the alumni list up to date.

I will continue to mail out cardboard crowns.

We need donations for our flower fund.

Thank you,

Ms. Charlotte Wilson

"No way! It's him! I just saw Tate Gilman get on our plane." Sophia bounced on her toes and peered over the crowd as she waited to board the flight to Beijing.

Anne looked up from her phone and rolled her eyes at her best friend. "You need to stop surfing the internet so much. It is affecting your imagination." She returned to the text she was composing to her mother: **Flight from Boston landed late. Waiting to board for China.**

"Just because you are the only woman in North America who isn't crushing on Tate doesn't mean I haven't seen him." She adjusted the heavy bag on her shoulder.

"It's hard to be enamored since I know him." Anne checked the alert from her dorm-alumni website, <u>MisadventuresInLove. com</u>. An artist who'd graduated eight years before her had just received the title "Miss Guided" for her adventures in Paris. Of all the websites she'd miss over the next few months, <u>MisadventuresInLove.com</u> was at the top. It was definitely the funniest. Someday Anne would do something crown-worthy. As long as it wasn't something stupid like becoming a stress-faced meme character, she'd take it. Silly goal to earn a paper crown with a "punny" title, but ever since her freshman year, when an alumnus had earned the title *Miss Spent*, earning a Miscellaneous crown had been a bucket-list wish. With her luck, she would get one for being lost in China and never making it back. Miss Placed? Miss Oriented? Miss Ing?

"I still don't believe you. You claim that one kid in your year-book, Bertram T. Gilman, is the same person. And even though somewhat chubby thirteen-year-old boys can "*Glow Up*" into hot men—like the guy who played the awkward wizard in the movie—I'm not buying it. But you know who I mean." Sophia waved her hand as if casting a spell. For someone who fluently spoke five different languages, Sophia was no good at remembering names.

"Neville Longbottom." Anne filled in for Sophia. Bertram's metamorphosis from his early teens really had been remarkable. Anne would not have recognized him had his bio not said he'd attended a Chinese-immersion junior high where he had become fluent in the language. The fact that the *B* in front of *Tate Gilman* stood for *Bertram* had been scrubbed from the internet. Anne supposed the creator of the most popular language apps in the universe had all the money he needed to scrub anything from the worldwide fishbowl. "I didn't say he didn't turn out more than fine. It's just that in my experience, his personality does not match his looks. I doubt it is him anyway. Why would a billionaire be on a commercial flight?"

"It is well-known Tate doesn't own a plane and hates flying. I still think you're wrong about his name being Bertram. There is a possibility that two people in the world are named Tate Gilman. Not the same person." Sophia rolled her carry-on forward to get a better place in line.

Anne tucked her ticket in between the pages of her passport. Ahead and behind her, several other twenty-somethings wearing bright yellow T-shirts like hers did the same. In fifteen hours, Anne would step foot in China for the first time since she was eighteen months old. The opportunity to teach English this summer was one she couldn't pass up. Visiting China had been on her bucket list since she learned to write. A dream supported by her parents. The only obstacle to returning had been her failure to learn Mandarin.

Overhead, the speakers crackled, and a garbled voice announced that their section of coach was ready to board. Anne followed Sophia down the Jetway. As they entered the plane, Sophia craned her neck to see into the first-class section, but the curtains were drawn and a flight attendant stood guard.

Sophia dragged her rolling bag behind her. "I know it was him. I'll prove it when we get off. He won't be able to get through customs much faster than we can. You'll see it's Tate and not your friend or junior high nemesis or whatever."

"With our yellow T-shirts, he'll know to avoid us. Nothing screams unattached female more than a T-shirt declaring 'I teach English' in two languages." Anne found her seat. The next fifteen hours of her life would be spent wedged between Sophia, who had the window seat, and Gwynn, a third-grade teacher from Rhode Island. It could be worse.

Sophia stuffed her bag under the seat in front of her. "Not everyone wearing a yellow shirt is an unattached female. Did you see the guy from Montana? He's going to be a vice principal at an immersion school next year. That's one fine cowboy for you. And then the Texan. I wonder if he speaks Chinese with an accent."

"He can't speak it as poorly as I do." Anne fished a pair of headphones out of her backpack.

"If you tried Tate Gilman's Lingo-mi app, you'd be speaking like a native in no time. It wasn't rated the best language app of the year for the past two years for no reason." Sophia ripped open the bag containing the airplane blanket and sleeping mask.

"Technically I am a native. I don't have an ear for languages." This conversation had replayed at least weekly since Anne had showed Sophia her junior high yearbook. Mathematics came easier to Anne than languages did. "My Chinese is barely passable.

And I have no reason to think it will get any better just because you consider the creator to be hotter than triple-fire salsa."

"I think it's a psychological block. You were so traumatized in seventh grade your brain refuses to believe you can learn a language." Clearly the online psychology course Sophia had taken last semester was clouding her judgment.

"I don't understand why everybody thinks I will pick up Chinese so easily."

"It probably has to do with your classic oriental profile and that long dark hair."

Anne rolled her eyes. Gwynn arrived at her seat and was attempting to find enough space for her carry-on overhead. "I'm not sure how I will live an entire summer out of a suitcase and a half. I'm going to have to throw everything away to bring home souvenirs."

Sophia leaned over Anne. "You and me both. And then there's Anne, who has only her backpack and her one checked bag."

"My one talent is being able to pack more things into less space than anyone else. I still say I could have condensed your stuff into one bag. And I have a carry-on inside my suitcase so I can bring back souvenirs." Anne didn't bother to point out that her skirts took up less room than Sophia's jeans.

"And singing," Sophia stage-whispered.

"I wish I had your talent for packing." Gwynn kicked her backpack under the seat in front of her. "It would come in handy next fall. The classroom they've given me has to be the smallest in the entire school, and my class size is up by four."

"My talent doesn't extend to squishing active students into a cramped space." Anne buckled her seat belt and turned her cell phone to airplane mode after not receiving a return text from her mom. "I can't believe they expect us to sleep on this flight."

"Did you see the accommodations in business class? If I were there, I could sleep." Gwynn pulled out a sleeping mask. "First class has make-down beds."

In the aisles, the flight attendants were pantomiming the safety instructions.

"I'm going to dream of a man in first class. That should help me." Sophia blew up a travel pillow.

"Me too. I'm sure I saw Tate Gilman get on the plane. I'd love to get my hands on those abs or in that hair." Gwynn's smile indicated that she had just as big of a crush as Sophia.

"I told you," said Sophia.

Anne refrained from rolling her eyes. "Maybe you can get his autograph, ask him what the *B* stands for."

Gwynn raised her brows and pulled her blanket up to her shoulders. "Wake me up when we are in China."

The plane taxied to the runway. Sophia shut the window and closed her eyes. Anne tried to find a comfortable spot in her seat without bothering either woman. Too bad she couldn't come up with even an imaginary crush to dream about.

Tate Gilman settled into his first-class compartment, the section of the plane that was his for the next several hours. If his security team hadn't insisted on his privacy, he would be back in business class. The make-down bed was a pointless extravagance. He could never sleep on flights. Memories of his sixth-grade science-fair project came back to haunt him whenever he was thirty-two thousand feet over an ocean. He knew all the statistics proving the safety of flight, but it never helped. Flying should be impossible. He'd proven it in elementary school.

Tate's life was a series of unexpected impossibilities: earning a scholarship to one of the country's top tech universities, turning it down to go to the state college, dropping out and developing the app that netted him his first billion within four years, and becoming the first billionaire with a fear of flying to conduct overseas business. Most people with his income had their own planes and never flew commercial. Tate refused to buy one because that meant he would have to fly more places to justify the expense of plane, pilot, and crew. Another thing most billionaires didn't have to do.

Money had turned his life upside down. Overnight, he'd gone from the geek no one claimed to the guy everyone wanted to know. People he didn't even know asked for endorsements, photos, and a chance to raise his posterity.

Today he was lucky. No one had recognized him boarding the plane. For a moment he thought one woman in the yellow-T-shirt group had, but when the other woman next to her didn't react, he figured he was safe. According to their shirts, the group was headed to China to teach English. He'd wanted to do that one summer years ago. That wouldn't work well with a bodyguard in tow. Only two accompanied him on this trip. Since he wasn't well-known in China, it would be enough.

An attendant stopped to offer him a drink and snack. Tate asked for the ginger ale and crackers. He'd learned from sad experience that eating anything heavier wouldn't agree with his constitution. One day he would get rid of the psychosomatic symptoms that plagued him whenever he flew.

Tate surfed through the onboard entertainment. The airline had a decent selection of Chinese-language films. He chose one he hadn't watched and settled back into his seat. In the background of the first scene, there were several people with yellow shirts like the group of teachers. One woman reminded him of his old classmate, Anne. But then, almost every oriental woman of a certain age did. Some day he would find her and apologize for being a clueless teen. In the meantime, he would continue his quest to prove how wrong he had been.

A sword-fighting scene caught his attention. Tate spent the next fifteen hours immersed in films and actively trying to forget where he was.

Tate yawned several times as they landed. He checked his watch. Now for the hard part—getting through customs and staying awake for at least five hours without caffeine.

A number of other planes must have landed about the same time. The line for customs snaked around the large room a half dozen times. Ensconced behind his sunglasses, he did his best to avoid attracting the attention of his fellow passengers as he inched forward. Two more customs stations opened, and the line moved forward at twice the pace. Ten more minutes and he could be out of this crowd.

Laughter came from the line behind him. Then a shout had him turning his head before he could think.

"Bertram! Bertram!"

A tall, red-haired woman in one of the yellow shirts was smiling at him. Next to her, a shorter Asian woman covered her mouth, her eyes wide with horror. It couldn't be—but his brain found no other explanation. "Anne?"

"I can't believe you did that!" Anne ducked behind Sophia and the teacher from Montana to get out of Tate's line of vision. "He said your name. I know he did." Sophia stepped back, clearing Tate's view of Anne.

"He is coming this way." Gwynn's statement was hardly helpful. Tate allowed passenger after passenger to pass him and the two men with him—business associates or bodyguards, maybe both.

Anne searched for a place to hide. For obvious reasons, there wasn't an exit on this side of customs. Ducking her head, she ignored the commotion as much as she could, though it was difficult with Sophia elbowing her. The others in her group had stopped talking and now monitored Tate's progress like rubberneckers on the interstate. Only this collision was in progress, her car spinning helplessly out of control. Anne prayed for a soft landing.

When Tate reached their group, Sophia stepped forward and extended her hand. The two men with him closed the ranks. "Mr. Gilman, so sorry to have bothered you. I bet my friend you were you, and she claimed your name is—"

He held up a hand to stop her. "Few people in the world know me as that. Anne?"

Left with no choice, Anne raised her head and plastered on her best teacher smile. "Hi."

He took another step forward, his bodyguards taking one back, as the line continued to move toward the row of glass-paneled booths. "I promised myself if I ever saw you again, the first thing I'd do—"

One of his associates tapped Tate on the shoulder. It was his turn to pass through customs. Anne let out a breath she hadn't realized she was holding. Whatever it was he had to say, she did not want to hear it. There was no way it could be good. The group separated as they went through separate customs desks. Anne let two people move in front of her in line, hoping that when they were done, Tate would be gone. The customs official checked her passport twice. Following Anne's adoption, her parents had taken the necessary steps to ensure she had US citizenship; however, her passport listed her city of birth as Lanzhou, China.

"If you are coming to find your Chinese parents, you will not. Too hard." The official handed her passport back.

"I'm only coming to teach English." Anne moved to the next part of the customs process and picked up her single bag.

The group of teachers had gathered with their luggage near a support column. Anne glanced around for Tate but didn't see him. Wheeling her suitcase behind her, she crossed the area to join the group. Halfway there, one of Tate's large friends stopped her. "Mr. Gilman would like a moment with you."

She pointed to her group. "I need to go with them. I can't risk getting lost." One reality of her life was her inability to get to where she planned on going by the most direct route.

"It will only take a moment. Tell one of them you will be back shortly." He crossed his arms. Had he not been with Tate, she would have run from the spot screaming for help.

"Let me see if I can." Anne spotted Sophie's red hair in the group and made a beeline for her friend.

"What's up with Burly Guy?" Sophie craned her neck.

"He says Tate wants a minute with me."

"The woman in the blue jacket told us to take fifteen to go to the bathroom and things before she gives us our assignments. Some teachers will need to board another plane, and some will take the train. Check in with her."

Anne confirmed that she had a few minutes and left her suitcase with Sophie.

She turned back to Tate's associate. "I have ten minutes." Tate had better appreciate that she was sacrificing her restroom break. She followed the man down the hall to where he opened a door revealing a small room with a table and two chairs resembling a TV police-show interview room.

Tate leaned against one wall. "Sorry about the room. I wanted to talk to you without the entire world listening."

The other man left, shutting the door behind him. Anne stiffened at finding herself alone in a room with the man who'd once crushed her preteen soul. The smarter thing to do would have been to tell the big guy she would not speak with Tate. He had said enough to last a lifetime.

She shifted her cross-body bag and looked at her watch. "I have three minutes." She wasn't going to give up her restroom break, after all.

When Tate pushed off the wall and stepped forward, Anne stiffened and scooted back, keeping the table between them. Not a good sign, but probably what he deserved. He pulled the folded piece of wide-ruled notebook paper from his wallet and held it out to her. "I've kept this with me for fifteen years—in case I ever saw you again. It's the apology I wrote that weekend"—under Grandpa's watchful eye and frowning face—"after I reamed you for ruining the project. Which you really didn't. Your research was stronger than mine. I wanted to blame someone else for our grade. And when you mispronounced...Never mind. Unfortunately, my grandfather died the day after I wrote it. When I returned to school a week later, you'd left." She made no move to retrieve the note, so he set it on the table near her.

"That's the paper you held up in that press conference last year. You claimed it was the reason you designed Lingo-mi, the reason for your success."

"If we had enough time, I would tell you the whole story, things I've never told the media. But I want you to know I am so sorry for what I said." He wondered if she remembered how he'd told her she was a fortune cookie short of a Chinese dinner and that his hamster was smarter than she was. "I was cruel, and I understand if you never want to talk to me again or even forgive me. When Mrs. Chen told me you left the school, I knew it was my fault, but I didn't know where to look for you. I tried finding you on the internet, but I didn't know your father's name, and the search engines weren't great back then. I heard you'd moved over the next summer, but Williams is far too common a name."

"So you have carried this apology around all these years?" Anne pulled the paper across the table toward her with one finger but didn't pick it up.

"I figured I shouldn't change my apology just because my vocabulary increased. I think my three minutes are up." Tate took a card from his pocket. "My number. I'd like to talk more." In his mind, this moment had always ended in a hug of forgiveness from the cutest girl in his seventh-grade class. But judging by the look on her face, he would be lucky to get a handshake.

"I thought you were angry because my friend yelled your name."

"It got my attention, and I finally found you." There had been no media present to record the moment. And no one had had a phone out videoing the customs line. If someone was going to reveal his first name, it was an ideal location.

"I'm surprised you didn't cyber-stalk me."

"I tried. But the correct Anne Williams is almost as impossible to find as Maria Garcia from kindergarten—too many to choose from."

Anne picked up the paper and put it in her bag. "Thanks for apologizing. I'd better go." She opened the door and disappeared into the hallway.

Mitch entered as soon as she left. "That didn't even take her full ten minutes."

"She had ten?"

"That's what she told me." Mitch shut the door.

Tate pulled out one chair. "It didn't turn out as I planned."

"Maybe you'll see her again. Your car is here. I don't know about you, but right now a hotel bed sounds like heaven." The head of Tate's foreign-security team's jaw clenched in a stifled yawn.

A clean bed and nine uninterrupted hours of sleep was all Tate's biological clock needed to adjust to the new time zone. But the chances of uninterrupted sleep with Anne on his mind were slim. Tate pushed himself up and followed Mitch to the waiting car. As they passed the group of yellow-shirted teachers, Tate noted that Anne was not among them.

*A*nne leaned her head against the stall's door and took three deep breaths to calm her nerves. After all these years. She peered inside her bag at the wide-ruled notebook paper. It looked old enough to be from the seventh grade. It probably said something lame like "I'm sorry. Do you forgive me? Yes or no?" complete with little check boxes. She held up the business card he'd handed her. On the back in neat handwriting, the kind architects used, he'd written his email address and a phone number. The email must be a private one as it started with Bertram@.

Anne stuck the card in the fold of the note. It might be another dozen years before she ran into him again or needed the number, but she wasn't about to leave it in an airport restroom garbage can, not with his private information on it. In China, you never knew who or what could be watching. One of her coworkers had told her of surveillance drones that looked like birds.

When her heart rate returned to normal, she checked her watch, then left the stall, pausing long enough to wash her hands. She left the restroom and walked—until she ran into a wall of doors with an unmistakable red icon meaning "Do not enter," so she retraced her steps and found the group of yellow-shirted teachers not a hundred yards from the restroom in the opposite direction.

By the time she reached the group, assignments had been passed out.

Sophia waved her over. "I have yours. We are at the same school in Xi'an, and our plane leaves in an hour. There are other teachers traveling with us, so we are all going to the gate together."

Thirty-five minutes later, as they sat in one corner of the waiting area, Sophia asked Anne about her meeting with Tate. "I told you it would work! Was he angry I called him Bertram?"

"I asked you not to. I nearly died of embarrassment when he asked Mr. Bodyguard to come get me."

"But he talked to you."

Anne wasn't sure how to feel knowing he'd wanted to apologize all those years ago. Even if he had spoken up then, it wouldn't have changed things. She would've left the immersion program anyway as her grades weren't good enough to stay. Even the one semester she had taken Chinese in college had been as disastrous as junior high. If there hadn't been a math option instead of foreign language, she would never have graduated from Bradford. The only discrimination she ever felt growing up was that her grades didn't fit the stereotype. Asian students were generally brilliant, and anything less than top grades in every subject was a disgrace. Every other student in her high school's Asian-American club had graduated with honors, not solid Bs. Some kids had even asked if she was mentally deficient. "Tate seemed glad you'd called his first name. He wouldn't have turned around to look if you hadn't. He claimed he wanted to apologize for what happened in seventh grade. He even had this note he claimed he's been carrying around for years."

Sophia turned from the window where she'd been watching the planes. "You are kidding me. No guy carries some note around for over a dozen years because he wants to apologize for being a preteen jerk. I don't think my brothers apologized for anything unless Mom was giving them the eye."

"I know, right? My brother would tell me he was sorry, then mumble 'not.' I can't even think of many women who would apologize years later. I still can't believe it. And it's the same note on every social media site in the universe, he claims is the whole reason he made the language app."

"No way."

Anne nodded but didn't show Sophia the note. As star crushed as she was, she would probably take it.

They sat in silence observing the bustling airport for a couple minutes. Even without the yellow T-shirts, the other members of their group would stand out. An odd sensation crept over Anne; this was the first time in her memory she'd ever sat in a place where most people looked like her. Yet beyond shared genetics, she had nothing in common with them. The only people at their gate she could identify or communicate with were the other teachers.

Sophia continued the conversation. "I think it makes sense. I mean, if he was trying to make up for being a jerk and making fun of your Chinese, he could have dreamed up Lingo-mi. Maybe he was trying to figure out a way to help you learn the language. But it is way odd. Have you ever tried Lingo-mi? I tried the Farsi one just for fun." Only a woman who picked up languages faster than kindergarteners picked up bugs could say that. Sophia should have worked for a spy agency; her language skills were wasted as a teacher at her immersion elementary school.

It was probably just her imagination, but Anne's bag seemed to grow warm where Tate's letter sat waiting to be read. Maybe tonight before bed—whenever that would be. In front of them, one of the male teacher's head bobbed. The time change must be wreaking havoc on his internal clock. Envy filled her. If not for Tate, she might sleep too.

Anne opened her school packet to learn they were going to be teaching in an elementary school next to an orphanage.

Sophia pointed to the photo printed on the description paper. "I suppose that one is much like the one you were in as a child?"

"I guess one orphanage is much like any other, but I have no memories before I was two." Anne had watched a documentary about an adopted woman who'd come back to China to find her birth family, a nearly impossible task. Unlike other adoptees she met, Anne never felt a pull to find her "real" parents. Mom and Dad were her parents in every way, just like Gareth, born in Madagascar, and Emilee, born in Romania, were her siblings, along with Katelyn, Dad's biological daughter from his first marriage. Mom always said family wasn't all hereditary since love was a choice.

Anne unzipped her cross-body purse. Bypassing the folded notebook paper, she pulled out a pack of gum and offered Sophia a piece. The note would wait.

The luxury suite catered to Western businessmen and high-end tourists. The light-blocking window blinds, comfortable bed, and neutral decor should have guaranteed him a good sleep. The news that they had a meeting this afternoon necessitated a nap. Instead, Tate found himself staring at the walls and wondering why they lacked personality. They were white and gray, with a print that could have come from a budget hotel in small-town USA. With the windows covered, he could be in LA or London—only the hotels he'd stayed in there boasted personality. Not that he'd noticed until it was missing. Even a low-budget seascape might take his mind off running into Anne. Things he wished he'd said echoed around his brain. He should have asked for her number or email or something. Then he could contact her when she returned home. Depending on her service provider, she might have access to her email while teaching, or to text. Or he could always wait for another twelve years. He was bound to run into her again.

Tate hadn't planned on giving the old note to her. The only

reason he'd had it in his hand was because he'd pulled it out of his wallet to read it one more time—the adolescent ramblings of a boy who'd suffered his first true crush. All school year, he watched her from afar. Well, from across the room. He loved the shrug she gave when she didn't know the answer, the way she tucked her hair behind her ear during a test when she was nervous, and the sound of her laugh when she and the other girls argued about which of the Jonas brothers was the cutest. Tate had tried to mimic the singing trio's haircuts, but his mother had refused to let him get his hair permed and ruined the only chance for his hair to be anything but straight and lifeless. He'd even auditioned for the school talent show. Mrs. Chen was all kindness as she told him she knew he had talents elsewhere.

He'd worked on the auto-tuner app he'd designed in college until he realized no amount of technology could give him tune and rhythm. After that, he'd poured his energy into creating an easy-to-learn language app. He'd run test after test on focus groups ranging from preschool to senior citizens, searching for a combination that allowed people to learn and remember the most difficult of languages. And he'd teamed up with game designers to make his teaching method fun and engaging. Every test he made, every prototype that failed, Tate had pulled out his seventh-grade yearbook and stared at Anne's grainy black photo, promising to help her learn the language of her birth country.

Now they were both in the same place—or had been. She could have been assigned to teach anyplace in the country. He'd noticed as the teachers received their assignments that some had plane tickets. Finding her again would take a miracle.

He'd apologized. That was all he wanted to do, right? So what if she was cuter now than she was at twelve? She'd almost smiled in the little conference room. What would a real smile look like? It didn't matter. She probably never wanted to see him again.

Tate rolled over, covered his head with the pillow, then counted backward from twenty.

His alarm woke him long before he was ready. He slid the dot to snooze. Before it went off again, Jared was pounding at his door. "Tate! Thirty-minutes!"

"Fine! Getting up. Nap time over." Tate scrubbed a hand over his face, disappointed he hadn't slept long enough to dream about Anne now that he'd met the grown-up version. There was nothing to do but to hope she called him. In the meantime, he needed to prep for his dinner meeting with the Chinese tech company eager to share in his vision of a more open China.

The bus won the award for the most painful form of transportation that day. Anne tried not to rub her aching back as she exited with Sophia in front of the gated school. A woman dressed in a spotless blue skirted suit stood stiffly near the entrance, flanked by an armed guard.

Anne and Sophia wrestled their suitcases off the bus and to the gate. The woman, who must be an administrator, frowned. Anne imaged how bad they looked after twenty-four hours of travel. Wrinkles everywhere. The quick tooth brushing she did on the plane barely counted as basic hygiene.

"You are Chinese." The woman glared.

"My passport says I am American." Granted, it listed her birthplace as China, but her parents had been diligent in completing the proper paperwork to guarantee her US citizenship.

"At least you use an American accent. Some companies try to pass off Cubans or Germans as American." The woman's English had a British accent and came off as snobbish as the stereotype. No doubt the supervisor went to a university in the UK. She turned to Sophia. "What about you?"

A wicked gleam sparkled in Sophia's eye as she answered in a deep Southern drawl. "Yes, ma'am, 100 percent Yankee."

Anne bit back a laugh. A Southerner would never call themselves a Yankee.

The woman stepped back. "I am Kim Lǎoshī. Lǎoshī is my title as a teacher, not my last name, which is Kim." The explanation was unnecessary as *Lǎoshī* was one of the few words Anne had ever gotten right in her immersion program. The company had also explained the title in her online orientation programs.

"Clyde, Sophia." Sophia stuck out her hand, no doubt to goad Kim Lǎoshī.

"Williams, Anne." Anne gave the slightest of nods, not sure if she should bow.

"I oversee our English education program. If you encounter any problems, bring them to me. I will show you your room in your dorm." Instead of entering the schoolyard, she walked down the street to the first building. "This is our teachers' dorm. As foreign teachers, we expect you to be in the dorm by 20:00, which is eight o'clock, every night, when you teach the next day. You do not teach on Saturday or Sunday, so you may stay out or even go touring, but you must be back by 20:30 on Sunday." She handed each woman a key card. "If you are late, these will not work. You will need a guard to come find me if you wish to gain readmittance. Don't lose the keys. There is a seven-hundred-yuan replacement fee."

Anne calculated the exchange rate. It was just over $100.

Kim Lǎoshī held the door while they wheeled in their suitcases. The guard who'd followed them down the street waited outside. Sophia glanced in his direction and rolled her eyes. "Does he follow us everywhere?" This time she spoke without an accent.

"No, he is here to protect you only at the school."

Anne shot Sophia a warning glance before any comments about prisons or protecting the school from American teachers spilled out of her mouth.

Kim Lǎoshī opened the door to a large dorm-style room that had two comfortable chairs, a television, and a mini fridge in addition to the expected beds. The space was larger than Anne expected. She pulled her bag into the room after Sophia.

"Breakfast is at seven thirty. You are later than we expected, so you missed dinner. I will ask for food to be sent up so you don't need to go find some. Tomorrow after lunch I will show you around. That should give you some time to sleep." Kim Lǎoshī closed the door behind her as she left.

"Do you suppose they lock us in?" Sophia claimed the bed nearest the window.

"I don't think you should try to find out. I can't believe you spoke to her with that accent." Anne opened one of the armoires in the room. She wouldn't be able to sleep unless she was unpacked.

"I was ticked that she was annoyed with you. Just because your genes say you are Chinese doesn't mean you aren't American." Sophia plopped her suitcase in the middle of the bed. "I reek. Do you mind if I take the first shower?"

"Don't you want to wait for dinner?"

A knock at the door announced that Sophia wouldn't need to wait. The woman at the door held out a tray and spoke in rapid Chinese. Sophia spoke a few words in Mandarin with her, then ended the conversation by thanking her. Anne was surprised she'd been able to pick out the words *rice* and *thank you* from the conversation—although the two steaming bowls of rice and vegetables on the tray may have helped with the vocabulary.

They ate in silence. Sophia set her empty bowl on top of the microwave and went to the shower. Anne rinsed both bowls and set them back on the tray. Perhaps the woman had told Sophia what to do with them. It only took her a few minutes to finish unpacking. Anne looked at her purse...Sophia typically took long showers. She should have enough time to read the note from Tate.

Sitting down on the center of the bed, she opened it. The creases were soft and worn, as if Tate had folded and refolded the note over the years. Anne smoothed it out on the bedspread.

The blue ink was faded but still legible.

Dear Anne,

I am sorry for what I said in class today. Grandpa says I was wrong to judge you because of your ancestry. I don't speak Swedish because I have blond hair. I would like to help you with your Chinese if you want. Grandpa says I should make people better with the talents I have, not hurt them because theirs are not the same as mine.

Please forgive me for calling you names and saying you are stupid. I should have done more on the assignment and helped you with your pronunciation.

Bertram Tate Gilman

PS. You have other talents, like when you sing in music class. Sometimes I can hear you, and it is pretty.

PPS. My grandpa died, and when I came back to school, you were gone. Chen Laoshi won't tell me where you went. I hope I can find you. I really, really need to say I'm sorry. I promised Grandpa I would, and a man doesn't break his promise. I also promised him I'd help you with your Mandarin.

The last line was in black ink rather than blue.

Anne read the note again. If he had given it to her in the seventh grade, she would have doubted the sincerity of the message. Having taken several child-development classes, Anne reasoned the note was better than average for a preteen male. Tate could have apologized without giving her the old note, which left him vulnerable to her ridicule or even her selling it at auction. It would be worth two- to three-years' worth of her teacher's salary. The full-name signature might even be worth a fourth year.

The water in the bathroom stopped running. Anne refolded the letter and slipped it back into her purse. The business card lay on her bed. She picked it up, curious. She wondered if she could find him on a Chinese texting app she'd downloaded before she came over. She typed his number in and was rewarded with a match to the screen ID "Bertram T."

Sophia opened the bathroom door. "I left you some hot water. The soap they have in there smells like lavender and ginger."

Anne turned off her phone and palmed the business card.

"Did you text home?" Sophia didn't wait for an answer. "Good idea. I should let Mom know I made it safely. You know what a worrywart she is. Every single time she's heard anything negative about China over the last six months, she's repeated it to me at least three times. With the time difference, Mom should have just eaten breakfast." Sophia pushed her suitcase aside and plopped down on her bed, thumbs flying.

Grabbing her pajamas and toiletries, Anne headed for the shower, phone still in hand.

She sent a quick message to her family on the group chat, letting them know she'd arrived safely in Xi'an.

Before she lost her nerve, she sent a quick text to Tate.

Thanks for the note and apology.

Her fingers hovered over send. It felt like she should say more, but other than a few months in their seventh-grade class, she didn't know him at all. She set the phone on the counter and tested the water. Lukewarm. Just like her unsent response.

Anne bit her lip and deleted the message.

These long meetings caused Tate's mind to wander. He counted fifteen wireless devices around the table where nine people sat. When it came to being paperless, China needed to share some of its practices with the rest of the world. Tate rarely saw anyone using paper for anything, even in meetings. Many Chinese apps were available worldwide, and though Google had been banned by the Great Firewall, its Chinese search-engine equivalent, Baidu, was accessible in the States. It wasn't the technology as much as the mindset. Admittedly, the Chinese were more attached to their phones than Americans.

Tate's partnering with a Chinese tech company would make the English learning version of his app widely available in China, helping bring the two worlds closer together. His team had spent months poring over every nuance of Lingo-mi to make sure that not a single word would raise objections on a religious or political note. With nearly one-third of the country learning English, Tate believed his app could tap the market, delivering English education to even the most far-flung provinces.

Tate waited for the interpreter to translate the last statement by the Chinese government representative, only half listening for a change in meaning. He didn't need an interpreter, but using one gave him time to process. It also allowed him to listen to the private conversations of the surrounding businessmen who were less guarded in their belief that he could not understand them. So far, not a single person had asked if he spoke Mandarin or Cantonese beyond the survival words, such as greetings and "Where is the bathroom?" He would have told the truth, in their own language. The little deception didn't bother him as he concluded after the first meeting that most of the people in the room spoke enough English to not need a translator in day-to-day conversation.

Tonight's dinner was a precursor to tomorrow's negotiations, a test to see if either side had moved from the position they'd taken during the last meeting three weeks ago.

By the time Tate and Jared returned to the hotel, they were both yawning. Jared turned the television to the English-language news channel to cover their lack of conversation. Tate pulled out a spiral notebook. One of Tate's rules in China was to assume he was always being watched and monitored. An initial sweep of the hotel room found two bugs planted so obviously that someone meant them to be found and removed—a task Mitch had completed upon their arrival. Rather than set them at ease, it put both men on alert. There would be more bugs, and perhaps even cameras, in less obvious spots.

As one of Tate's oldest friends, Jared was far more than a bodyguard. But Jared didn't want the role of vice president or a seat on the board. He hadn't even cashed in his stock, which made him a major shareholder. Jared preferred to keep the things the way they had been at college—with the two of them planning and Tate getting the credit. The role of bodyguard gave Jared access to every meeting without question, and no one ever guessed Jared was more than he pretended to be.

"What did you think of dinner?" Tate asked as he wrote his real question on the paper.

The government rep kept testing me to see if I understood Chinese. I suppose they did a thorough background check. Did you learn anything?

As fluent in Chinese as Tate, Jared nodded as he said, "I enjoyed the rice."

They have their own app, though it doesn't work as well. They would pirate, but they want your face on the app. Those blond roots of yours get them every time.

"Rice? Really?"

I think they will offer us the contract tomorrow.

Better get it thoroughly checked.

"I'm particular about my rice."

The conversation wasn't meant to be titillating, but they may have reached an all-time low with a conversation about rice. Tate moved to a topic he wanted them to know about. "Have you heard anything from the office about the charity project?"

Jared scrolled through the phone. "No, we have four orphanages to check on. You know they will be showing us their best face, don't you?"

"Of course they will. That is why we will look at the shoes. They may put the children in their best clothing, but they won't spend money on new shoes." Tate stifled a yawn to cover his smile. If someone were listening in, the children in all four of the orphanages he'd filed in his travel plans would have new shoes by noon tomorrow.

Jared wrote one word on the paper. *Anne?*

Tate shook his head. During dinner, he'd received a notification that she wanted to connect on the chat app, which he'd approved. However, she'd never sent a message. He would wait a day to see if she did or if she severed the connection. It was possible she didn't realize that in looking him up she had inadvertently requested contact with him. "I think I will turn in. Good night."

Alone in his room, Tate checked the chat app one last time. Maybe it was just as well she hadn't messaged him yet. He assumed the Chinese chat app wasn't as private as it looked. When he saw Anne again, he would give her a copy of the prototype app his team had developed for foreign businessmen who wanted a secure line while inside China. No government official need know more about his social life, or lack thereof, than Tate did.

This time when he closed his eyes, he slept.

reakfast included scrambled eggs served with tomato slices in a small dining area on the main floor of the dorm. Anne had hoped for something more traditional. She'd wanted to try jianbing, the local equivalent of crepes.

Several uniformed teachers walked past Sophia and Anne and nodded, but none stopped to talk on the way to their tables. Anne caught an occasional whispered word or two from the conversation around her, but from Sophia's frown, it was clear her friend understood more of the conversation. With nowhere else to go, they returned to their room.

Anne pulled up the chat app and filled her family in on her travels.

Sophia opened her suitcase to move the contents to her armoire. "In case you didn't catch it, you were the major topic of conversation this morning."

"Just me?"

"They were trying to figure out how American you are—if both parents were Chinese or if you were born here and then adopted."

Seriously? She was being discriminated against? "I don't understand why it matters, other than the children's perception. They may listen to you better because you are a mesmerizing redhead."

"More likely because I am speckled. Do Asians get freckles?"

Anne shrugged. "I don't. Some do. I read an article about Asian models embracing their freckles. They don't show up as easily as yours do."

"The joys of being so pale I practically glow in the dark." Sophia opened her mouth wide to make a ghostly face.

There had been a time when Anne envied the fair skin of her friends and European-born sister. But Mom and Dad had helped her embrace her own beauty. She particularly liked her hair. It lay nicely even when she didn't have time to blow it dry. "Your red hair attracts men almost as fast as a free ticket to a Red Sox game."

Sophia tossed her hair. "It is good for that, isn't it? But it doesn't dye well. I tried once in junior high. At least it didn't turn green." She set her suitcase on top of the armoire. "Do you mind if I close the blinds? I could use a couple more hours of sleep."

"Not at all." Anne texted the answer to her sister's question about turbulence during the flight.

"Who are you texting?"

"My family."

"Not Tate?"

"No. Why would I do that?"

"Because he gave you his number?"

"How do you know that?"

"I didn't. But you just confirmed it." Sophia pulled her blanket up and plumped her pillow. "You'd be an idiot not to text him back."

"Why? I don't want to start a relationship."

A long pause filled the space. "You never know when you'll need a friend." Sophia yawned and rolled over.

Anne answered a question about the food on the flight over and bid her family good night, as it was around midnight at home.

Bertram T was at the top of her contact list. She tapped his name and rewrote the text she'd erased last night.

Thanks for the apology. It was longer than I expected. :)

This time she hit send before she could talk herself out of it. A reply came a moment later.

—Glad you read it. What do you mean longer?

I expected one of those yes-or-no check-box notes: Do you forgive me? Yes or no?

—I remember those. Are you teaching yet?

No, our first classes will be on Monday.

— Where did you end up?

A suburb of Xi'an. One of the residential schools.

— That is where the Terracotta Army is, isn't it?

Yes, I can't wait to see them. It is the first thing on my Chinese bucket list.

— You have a bucket list just for China?

Of course. If I am going to be here for three months, I want to see as much as I can.

— I thought most teachers stayed longer.

Not with our program. We teach at the elementary school for six weeks and then at one of the college immersion camps for four weeks. There is one week in the middle for sightseeing and another at the end.

—Then what do you do?

Go home

—Where?

Anne read the question again. Why did he want to know? Was it just a conversation thing or did he really want to know?

Massachusetts. I teach second grade.

She volunteered the last part to avoid another question. It must have done the trick as no immediate reply came. She looked at the conversation. All the questions were from him. She'd promised herself after the interpersonal communications workshop to ask other people more about themselves. Obviously she was failing. With over two hours until they had to meet Kim Lǎoshī, Anne decided Sophia had the right idea.

As she lay down, her phone pinged.

— If I came to Xi'an next weekend, would you see the warriors with me?

"Wait? What?"

Sophia stirred in her bed. Anne covered her mouth to prevent herself from saying anything else out loud. Sophia would freak out if she knew Tate Gilman had just asked her out.

I have to check with Sophia, my roommate. We were going to go together.

—No problem. Jared, one of the guys who was with me, will be coming.

I'll let you know.

—Sounds good. Can we chat later? I have a meeting …

Anne almost wished Sophia was awake so she had a sounding board. But she knew what Sophia would say. Anne typed her answer and hit send. Then she pulled up her book app. No way would she be able to sleep after that exchange. But maybe she could block it out in an imaginary world.

—Yes.

Tate had only a moment to school his reaction before walking into the conference room. He sat down and wrote Jared a quick note.

Rearrange schedule to do Xi'an orphanage on Friday. Visiting warriors next Saturday +2 on tickets.

He folded the note before passing it to Jared. The government official closely watched the exchange. Tate wished he had the edible paper bakeries used for photo cakes. If Jared could just eat the note…

The man at the head of the table stood and began to speak in lightly accented English. "After much deliberation, we would like to partner with you to make your app available to our citizens. I let my niece use it last weekend when she was home from school, and her English improved in just a day. Shall we work on the contract?"

"I would be honored to work with your company. What are your terms?"

By lunchtime, a tentative contract had been negotiated and sent to lawyers on both sides to work out the details. The government official participated in another round of handshakes and bows before excusing himself. Tate assumed he'd left with a copy of the contract. They went to a nearby restaurant to celebrate. Mitch replaced Jared as bodyguard. Hopefully he could find a place to call the States without being eavesdropped on. As far as Tate could tell, their hosts had not realized that Jared played more roles than merely acting as a bodyguard to an American tech mogul.

As they ate, Tate looked around the restaurant. If possible, people here seemed even more attached to their phones than Americans. It was easy to tell those who were dining for business, like the men at his table who'd stored their phones in their pockets and out of sight. Over a dish featuring duck, arrangements were made to meet again Monday to sign the final legal documents.

"Would you like a tour guide to show you our city for the next two days?" offered the CEO.

Tate responded in Mandarin. "Thank you for your kind offer, but I already have my days planned."

"You speak Chinese very well for an American. Why did you not tell us?"

"You didn't ask. Considering that the original version of my app only taught Mandarin, I thought you would know."

The man bobbed his head. "Your knowledge of our language kept your negotiating from a strong position hearing all our conversations not just what we translated. We used interpreters when we did not need them either. As you Americans say, 'Well played.'"

"Since we are to be partners, it is good to know that language is not a barrier." There had been enough barriers during the past months of exploring the partnership. The fact that Tate refused to drink had caused no end of problems during his first visit. Only after seeing this was a firmly held value did trust form. For his part, Tate failed to see how conversations over drinks built relationships.

Mitch and Tate headed back to the hotel. Jared's bags sat by the door, packed and ready. "I was able to reschedule as you asked. But we need to catch a 17:00 plane to Nanjing to be there for the tour in the morning. They were not excited about changing dates as they were busy distributing shoes today."

Tate exchanged high fives with the other men. Next time he would have to ask for something bigger.

As he packed, he checked his wallet. The empty space where he'd kept his apology note gave him pause. For years, that note had been his link to Anne. He pulled a spiral notebook out of his bag, wrote a note, folded it, and put it in the empty spot. Someday he hoped to share this note with Anne, too.

Kim Lǎoshī led them through the hallways of the school and into a small computer lab. "On these computers you will find the lesson plans of the teachers who just left. Do either of you sing?"

"I do." Anne earned herself another glare.

"What about you?" Kim Lǎoshī addressed Sophia.

"Not well."

"Sing a children's song," demanded the teacher.

Anne mentally cataloged the songs she'd sung with her students. Dropping anything patriotic or religious, she settled on a counting song. As she sang, Kim Lǎoshī's face softened.

"You sing very well. Perhaps you can help some of our preschool children from the orphanage over the back wall. They are hosting a distinguished American visitor next week. We have been trying to teach them some songs for a presentation. But our music teacher's English is not as good."

"I'd be glad to help."

Kim Lǎoshī offered her first smile of the day to Anne. "After we finish here, I'll show you our music room. Use your key card to turn the computers on. You don't need a password. The old lesson plans are in folders by grade. Sit down and see."

Anne and Sophia sat down at the computers and swiped their key cards over a black pad. The screens sprang to life and welcomed them by name. No way would Anne use this computer for email. Not that she trusted email to be sent privately from China after reading blogs where emails home arrived with sentences redacted or not at all. Politics and religion seemed to be the biggest triggers.

The lessons were well organized and fully planned. It was more than she expected to find based on the blogs of previous teachers. She had prepped some of her own lessons before coming and brought the necessary supplies. After a few minutes, Kim Lǎoshī began to fidget.

Sophia turned from her computer. "How do we log out?"

"Just tap your keycard again."

Once the computers were powered down, they watched some of the classrooms through the windows in the doors. These students were more attentive than the ones Anne taught back home, but she expected increased attentiveness since teacher, or lǎoshī, was a respected title in China. If only the same thing could happen in the US, maybe parents wouldn't spend half of parent-teacher conference arguing that their little darling couldn't possibly be the one with low scores or throwing the mud ball on the playground. They stopped at the music room. Rows of little violins lined the shelves on one wall. "Do either of you play an instrument?"

Sophia counted off on her fingers. "Flute, bassoon, piano, and viola, only not well."

"I play the piano." Anne hadn't wanted to learn to play anything else after her first year of lessons, afraid to find another instrument competing with her first love. Whenever she visited her parents, she played their baby grand for hours.

"Good. You play, and you sing." Kim Lǎoshī pointed at Sophia, then Anne.

Sophia looked at the music sitting on the piano. "Cool, they have some Disney songs. How about 'Let It Go'?"

Anne didn't remember all the words, mostly because her dorm mates had created a few parodies of the songs in college, her favorite being "Let Him Go"—the perfect breakup song. She stood behind Sophia at the piano.

Kim Lǎoshī nodded her approval. "Maybe you will work well, after all. You sing like an American, too. Singing is very important in teaching. I will tell the principal he should not send you back."

Anne caught Sophia's eye. Was the woman serious? They would have sent her back over genetics? Was that a big deal everywhere or only at this school? It seemed like the recruiting company would have told her before accepting her application. Her DNA would have been hard to miss in the video she'd sent in.

They returned to the main hall. "Sometimes the children want to talk to you. You may talk with them in the courtyard or the main rooms. You are not allowed in their dorms unless I accompany you. Dinner is served in the teacher-housing dining room Monday through Thursday. Friday, Saturday and Sunday, you buy your own. There are many good places and vendors nearby, and it is a short subway ride to the famous Muslim Quarter. You can also rent bikes if you have the app. Easy to get around Xi'an. I will see you Monday morning at 9:00 a.m. The schedule is in the computer. Be prepared."

Sophia held up her key card. "Computer lab?"

"Sounds like we'd better look at the old lesson plans. I noticed a few computers over in the dorm lobby. Do you suppose they work the same?"

Sophia opened the computer lab door. "Maybe. But I doubt we can use them for anything other than school. It isn't like we can watch Netflix. Although we might be able to stream *High School Musical*, Shanghai version."

"I don't think I know enough Chinese to enjoy that without subtitles."

"You should try Tate's app." Sophia sat down on one of the computer-lab chairs. "You do have it on your phone, right?"

"I don't see how an app can help me. I'm just not a language person like you."

"That's the whole point." Sophia rolled her eyes. "Our entertainment choices after 20:00 are limited to Chinese TV or the gazillion books I know you have downloaded to your phone. I say try it for an hour a night."

Using his app meant thinking about him and the weird conversation they had this morning. "Speaking of Tate, he will be in Xi'an next weekend and wants to go see the Terracotta Army with us." She sat at the computer next to Sophia's.

"With us or just you?"

"Us. He said his bodyguard would be with us too. So it is kind of—"

"A double date. Why didn't you tell me when he first asked you out?"

"I don't think it is a date, exactly."

"Let me see the texts, and I'll tell you." Sophia held out a hand.

Anne weighed the consequences of not handing over the phone. Either way, there would be pain involved. She placed it in Sophia's hand.

"Unlock it?" Sophia raised her brows.

After opening her chat app and the conversation with Tate, she handed the phone back.

"Read *it*? Read what?"

"An apology note he wrote in the seventh grade. I am not going to let you read and analyze it. Just move on."

"Wow. That is a date. I think I should say I can't go."

"If I go, you go. Tate, his bodyguard, and me is not a date. It is a chaperoned visit to a bunch of pottery men."

"I can distract the bodyguard and give you some alone time."

"Alone with the other couple thousand people visiting the site. So it isn't really a date, just going out with an old friend."

"It sounds like a date, it looks like a date, and I bet when he shows up it will even smell like a date."

Anne took her phone back. "Look, I found the teaching schedule. We are in the same classes about half the day."

"You need to text him back and say you'll go."

"I was talking about our teaching." Anne scrolled through the week's scheduled classes. Some had links to specific lesson plans.

"No, you were avoiding the subject."

Anne swung around to glare at Sophia. "I don't see how. I am in China to teach."

"And the hottest tech billionaire in the world just asked you out. Where are your priorities?"

"I don't know…my contract, maybe?" Anne turned back to her computer and muttered, "And he isn't the hottest billionaire."

"I heard that, and if he isn't, who is?"

"I don't know, but if we were in the States, I would google it and find one." Anne opened the folder for her first class and skimmed the notes. The preschool class looked easy. Nursery rhyme songs and letter recognition. Next week was the letter *R*.

"Look, Baidu has an English version. When I type 'hot tech billionaire,' look who comes up."

Anne glanced at the screen. "Ha! He's listed below the Asian man."

"Not technically. The Asian has a net worth of only half a billion. So, say it. Tate is the hottest tech billionaire out there."

"Not too hard when there are only a handful of billionaires in the world."

Sophia rolled her eyes again. "What-ev-er. Just text him back."

Anne opened her phone. "Why are we friends?"

"Because you love me."

Anne showed her text to Sophia before she sent it.

We can go next Saturday. Thanks for the invitation.

Jared had groused because there wasn't a multibedroom suite in the local hotel they'd checked into. Mitch was worried more about security than he needed to be, and he walked around the entire perimeter before declaring that Tate could have the center room. The man who'd followed them from Beijing had disappeared into the hotel bar. Tate doubted Jared or Mitch were needed. Either the local government would protect him as soon as the man called them or they would protest his presence. Either way, it didn't matter. He was counting down the moments until he had a semblance of privacy and could answer the text that had popped up from Anne as soon as his phone was clear of the plane.

Jared ordered a dinner for them through the hotel clerk, who seemed shocked over Jared's fluency in Mandarin. Tate took his key and headed for his room. Mitch conducted a quick search of the room and found no bugs, but that didn't mean they were not there. Jared walked in with dinner just as Mitch finished his sweep of the other rooms. The three ate around the table and discussed their plans for the next day. The orphanage they hoped to visit was only a half mile away. Tate wanted to walk but knew arriving by car would make a better first impression.

A French couple who had long passed retirement age ran this orphanage and wished to return home for their last few years together. Theirs was one of a handful of orphanages not state run. Funds were always in short supply, yet reportedly the children were healthy and progressing as far as they could. Many of the children were unadoptable because of the various physical and mental disabilities. More than wanting to know if his newly formed charity could help them, Tate wanted to know what methods the couple had used so he could duplicate their success. Once their plan was outlined and with dinner finished, Jared and Mitch left Tate alone.

Tate moved to the bed and opened the chat app.

I'm glad you can make it work. How was your day? He waited only a few moments before the reply came.

— Fine. I am not sure the woman over the English program likes me very much. Apparently I am not supposed to speak good English because I wasn't born in the USA.

He had no reply for that one. It hit a little too close to his own opinion years ago. **I heard they preferred the Barbie- and Ken-doll types for teachers.**

— I missed that in the orientation packet.

If you knew, would you have still come?

—Yes. I have wanted to see China forever, and using my summer break is a good way to do that. Plus I get paid. I was just surprised, and I am still a bit upset.

Am I making it worse?

He had to know. If he was, he would do something. He had no idea what, but it would be something. The minutes ticked by.

— No. I think getting your letter and apology helped. I can put things in perspective. You aren't the only reason I left the program. My grades were suffering. I think Chen Lǎoshī put us together so you could help as you were—I mean are—so brilliant. I wasn't happy there. I was attending a different school than my siblings. They were not in an immersion program because there wasn't one in Romanian or Malagasy. Anyway, if you had helped me, it would have just delayed the inevitable. But knowing you wanted to apologize back then helps. It gives me hope that I can change the supervisor's mind about my ability to teach English. So thank you again. How was your day?

Good. After months of negotiation, I think we finally have a partner, but that could all fall apart when the lawyers work the contract over this weekend. Boardrooms are aptly named, in my opinion. I am so bored when I am in them.

— So, what is keeping you in China for the week?

Tate paused. Telling her about the orphanages would lead to questions he didn't want to answer, as, like his app, his reasons centered around an adolescent crush he'd never gotten over. **Mostly business. I also wanted to get some sightseeing in. Seems** like whenever I'm here, all my time is eaten up by negotiations.

—What if the same thing happens next weekend?

I'll walk out of the room and end them. I don't need my product here. The Chinese people needed it, though. I've seen their English-teaching apps.

—That sounds pompous.

I don't mean to brag, but I think the app is that good. Have you ever tried it?

—I downloaded it.

Tate smiled at her answer. Not what I asked.

—I don't think it would help me. I tried taking Mandarin in college. My worst grade. Lowered my GPA irreparably.

Do you want to speak Mandarin? There was another long pause before she answered.

—I did …mostly so I could have a connection to my heritage. But maybe eating dim sum is enough.

Will you try my app for just one week?

— What if I still fail? You'll be disappointed.

If you fail, I'll take you out to ice cream after the warriors.

— And if it works?

Then you can order the ice cream. I'll just pay.

—So I get ice cream either way?

Only if you try. *Please, I need to know if this works for you.* If she didn't want to learn Mandarin, that changed things and his promise to Grandpa would no longer be valid. But if she still wanted to learn, he wanted to help.

— To be honest, I promised my roommate I'd try your app. She thinks it is wonderful, but she picks up languages faster than a four-year-old picking up spilled M&Ms. I opened it on the plane and played with it for a bit.

Let me know how it goes.

—One condition: I don't have to report at all until next Saturday.

Done. But I hope we can text between now and then.

— I think I can fit you in. I probably should get to bed. Sophia is

making a big production about me still having a light on.

Good night.

— Good night.

Tate turned off his phone. It was the very best of nights.

*A*nne sat on a kiddie chair surrounded by two- to four-year-olds. Teaching them the welcome song wasn't going as well as she hoped. After three days of practice, they still wouldn't sing for her. Apparently her DNA got to even the little ones.

Sophia spoke from behind the piano. "We could switch places and do the Milli Vanilli thing."

"Do you think they'd notice?"

"It's worth a try."

Sophia moved the group closer to the piano. They tried again. This time the children sang. Sophia spoke to them in Mandarin. Anne only caught a few words, like *sing* and *piano*. Sophia stood. "I explained that I accompanied on the piano better, so we wanted them to sing with you. I also told them that even though you don't look American, you are and to close their eyes and listen and you would sing an American song."

"Thanks, I think." Anne moved back to the little chair as the first notes of the song played. She used her hands to cover her eyes and said the word *eyes* in Mandarin. All the children did the same thing. Then they sang the welcome song together. By the time they finished, half of them were peeking through their fingers, but they still belted out the song.

"Now with your eyes open." Sophia repeated the instructions in Mandarin.

Anne recognized all the words but missed the cue to come in. Sophia played the intro again. The children sang it perfectly. Both women praised them as their caregivers entered the room to take the children over to the orphanage.

Kim Lǎoshī entered the room. "What is a Milli Vanilli?"

"They were singers before we were born. They really didn't sing their songs, though. They lip-synched them." Anne answered as she stacked the chairs.

"That was a superb idea. They must be perfect for the important American donor. I have an invitation from the director of the orphanage. He asks that you sing. American donor must be impressed with our program. It is a great honor to be included in this special evening. Show that we work well with Americans." Kim Lǎoshī's tone didn't make it sound like a request.

"Is there any other music other than the Disney songs?"

Kim Lǎoshī walked over to a large file cabinet and pulled on a drawer, but it held fast. "I'll go find the keys."

"I know what you can sing." Sophia played the first few notes of Christina Perri's "Human." When Anne hesitated, Sophia rolled her eyes. "Don't tell me you forgot it."

Anne bit her lip. "You know what happened last time I sang that."

"Hello? You had a 102-degree fever. They still gave you great marks even though you didn't get on the show. Half the people there didn't do as well."

"Nor did they pass out in front of the judges." Anne's chance at stardom had been thwarted by some virus one of her students had brought to school.

"Just try it." Sophia played the opening notes again.

Anne sang the way they'd practiced a gazillion times. When she finished, there was clapping from the doorway. Four or five teachers stood behind Kim Lǎoshī. "You found the music?"

"No, I had that memorized."

"That song is perfect. I will tell the director. Don't forget to wear very nice dress. Not school uniform." Kim Lǎoshī left the room, and the other teachers followed.

"How did that happen?" Anne draped herself over the back of the piano.

"Face it. You are awesome."

"So now I get to sing in front of some donor to the orphanage? What do I even wear?"

"It's only six. There has got to be a shop you can buy a simple black dress at, although one of your maxi skirts would do." Sophia gathered her bag and hurried from the room.

Anne followed. A dress wouldn't make everything better. The stage fright that had come with her collapse at the auditions had never quite gone away. This performance could only be for a dozen people or so—probably some American church ladies. She'd sung a solo last Easter. Church ladies she could handle.

Legal is still dealing with the contract, I am visiting a small town near Dongguan. How is your day?

Tate hoped Anne would reply quickly. He wanted to forget most of his day. The orphanage he'd visited today needed help by way of a new administration. No amount of money could help when you had that kind of corruption. Only half the children had received new shoes, unlike in the other orphanages he'd visited.

When he and Jared had played that trick on the unseen listeners in the Beijing hotel room, he'd never expected that the ploy would help him in his quest to determine which orphanages would administer funds properly. The best thing he could do in this case was to alert the authorities to the problem. Though, since it was a private facility, he had no idea what local government could do.

His phone pinged.

—The children were wonderful. They're working hard to pronounce the words like I do. I spent most of my day in the lower grades. I can't believe how well they listen. They may spoil me for my class at home.

You would stay here?

—No, I don't think it would work for me. I have researched it, and most schools would not pay me as much as they would Sophia because of the DNA thing. I'd also miss my family and hamburgers.

In that order? Tate couldn't resist teasing her.

—Not necessarily. Hamburgers don't text me, so I miss them more.

So, would you miss me? Tate tried to come up with something else to type. Is that all you'd miss?

— Of course not. What about you? What would you miss?

I miss my pre-app life. Going to the movies. Here I am just another American, mostly. That wasn't what she'd asked, but it was the first thing that came to mind.

— I never thought about it. I guess money changes things.

Sometimes it makes it hard to know who your friends are. Sometimes people just want to be close to the money. Other people avoid me because of it.

— So you get judged on your money like I do my DNA?

Perspective. I never thought of it that way.

— There was a time when I wished you could feel all the pain I felt. But I am sorry you get to experience that.

Karma. And you don't need to apologize. I was a thirteen-year-old jerk.

— You were a disappointed thirteen-year-old whose brain hadn't fully developed.

I was a thirteen-year-old with a crush on the cutest girl in the school. Tate's thumb hovered over the send button for a moment before he let the message go. After four nights of texting, the crush was still there. He wanted to be more than friends, and getting it out now was better than after months of messaging and the few visits he could manage with her in China.

— Are you saying you had a crush on me?

Yup. And I may not be recovered yet.

— Oh. I'm not sure what to say.

How about we give it time? See if this friendship goes anywhere?

— I can do that. I enjoy our text conversations.

Just text wisely. I saw a woman riding a bike while looking at her phone at the same time the other day. She ran right into a car.

— We went shopping tonight, and I couldn't believe how many people ran into things. The entire country is like a teenager with his first phone. They never look up.

I wish … Tate deleted it. He had already revealed too much tonight. Jared would tell him he was moving too fast, letting old feelings and assumptions get in the way. I should say good night. It is late.

— Have a good night. I'll see you in two days.

Night.

Tate plugged his phone in and scrolled back through the conversation. Not how he'd intended it to go, but maybe it was for the best. Set clear expectations now rather than figure out later that the woman wanted to be "just friends." Prom date, first girlfriend, first kiss—all of it had ended in the friend zone faster than last year's stock-market dive. He read the conversation again and wished he could have a do-over. He shouldn't have confessed his crush. They had only been texting for a few days!

Jared was right when it came to women. Tate fell on the low side of the bell curve. He should change his chat-alert sound to one of the falling-bomb sounds like Wile E. Coyote going over the edge of the cliff.

$\mathcal{A}$nne's hands shook as she smoothed the black dress over her hips, though, thankfully, the woman in the mirror didn't look as scared as she felt. She hadn't sung in public since the night she'd fainted onstage at the Sing4Life tryouts. Church didn't count. Even if you were off-key, parishioners would still pat you on the head and declare they hadn't heard anything better in their life.

Sophia pounded on the bathroom door. "Ready? We need to go. Do you need another lecture?"

No! Certainly not another you-got-this-girl talk. It only made things worse. "Just a second." Anne opened her chat app and clicked on Bertram T. **I am doing something tonight that really scares me. Can you please send positive thoughts my way?** She wanted prayers, but religion wasn't something she could ask about in a text.

—Dangerous?
Only if I faint.
—Details?
Maybe later. If I don't die of embarrassment.
— Okay. Sending good thoughts for your very vague night.
Thanks.

Taking one last deep breath, she opened the bathroom door. "Let's get going."

Kim Lǎoshī met them in the lobby. "I have talked to the director. He wants the children to sing to the dignitary as soon as he comes into the room. They will use piano only, and one of the matrons, or "aunties," as we call them, will lead them as she did in today's practice." They exited out the back door and into the schoolyard. "The director will say a few words, and then Williams Anne, you will sing. Then I will bring you back to the dorm. It is Friday, so you have no curfew. I will see you again on Sunday night."

They followed Kim Lǎoshī out of a small gate and into a courtyard containing playground equipment, then entered the door to the kitchen of the orphanage. The room was hospital clean. Normal? Or in preparation for the visit? All the orphanage children who were at the school seemed clean and well-fed. Anne hoped it was normal. Kim Lǎoshī ushered them into a large room. Someone had pushed the furniture back to create a space at one end. An electric keyboard sat in the corner. "You two sit there."

A moment later, two aunties ushered two straight lines of children into the room. One auntie addressed Sophia. "Practice once."

Sophia played the introductory notes. Anne froze. The keyboard had a tinny sound. How could she sing to that? Sophia raised her brows. "Try to turn off some of the effects as I play."

Anne pushed several buttons as the children ran through the song, and the tinny sound disappeared, the keyboard sounding much more piano-like. The children exited the room. Sophia looked at Anne and shrugged as she played the first few lines of a popular ballad before Kim Lǎoshī frowned and shook her head.

Sophia leaned over. "I think you fixed it."

Anne nodded and closed her eyes, searching for a calm place. The orphanage director entered the room followed by the school's principal and others. To stave off stage fright, Anne focused on the keyboard. Sophia tapped her leg. Anne looked up. The first thing she noticed were the blue eyes of Tate Gilman. *I'm going to faint.*

Sophia pinched her leg, hard. "You've got this. You've texted him all week long. He is a friend, just like me."

Nope, not even remotely a friend like Sophia. This friend wanted to start a relationship with her.

The director of the orphanage stood in front of the room and began to speak, the two lines of children marching back into place as Sophia played an introduction to their song. When they finished, three of the children recited poems. The children bowed and the matrons ushered them out of the room. The director stood and spoke. Anne only caught a word here and there: *orphan ... adoption ...success.* The director turned to Anne and nodded. Sophia nudged Anne. *I've got this.* She walked to the center of the stage area and nodded at Sophia to play the single note that matched the first word. Anne made it through the first line and into the second, and then the people in the room faded as she hit the chorus and found the place where she melded with the music. The last note faded, and she gave a bow. Clapping filled the room. Tate and his bodyguards stood, as did the others. Anne bowed again. There was no curtain to hide behind, so she walked back to the keyboard where Sophia was also standing and clapping. "I knew you could do it."

Kim Lǎoshī beckoned the women from a side door. Anne didn't look back at the room, where the director was speaking again. As soon as they were around the corner, Sophia grabbed Anne's arm. "Did you see his face?"

"No, I just saw the music." Music was movement and life, and when Anne played or sang, she hid from the world inside the flowing shapes the music made around her.

"Girl, that man is—"

"Anne!" Tate's call stopped her as she entered the kitchen. She turned to see him jogging down the hall, followed by the director. "That was amazing. Why didn't you tell me you were singing?"

"Why didn't you tell me you were in Xi'an visiting orphanages?" Anne crossed her arms as the adrenalin rush from the performance faded.

"Touché. Some things are hard to explain on a text."

Anne nodded, aware that everyone was staring. "I should go." She turned.

He stopped her with a touch on the arm. "Chat tonight?"

"Sure." Anne turned and followed Kim Lǎoshī out of the building.

"You didn't say you knew American billionaire." Kim Lǎoshī's voice sounded harsher than usual.

"It wasn't relevant. We are just old acquaintances."

Kim Lǎoshī opened the back door to the dorm with her key card. "No, he looked at you like a man who wants to marry woman. He better still donate to orphanage. A private orphanage like our school needs money." The teacher spun around and left the building.

Sophia huffed. "I don't know what upset her, unless it was the director's insinuation that you were a product of their orphanage who returned to help them."

"Where did he get that idea? I wasn't adopted out of Xi'an." Anne wished more than ever that she could have understood the director's introductory words.

"Does Tate know that?"

"Maybe. I gave a presentation on Lanzhou, the town I came from, in our seventh grade class. My words could have been mixed up, but my map was right. But I doubt he remembers." As Anne headed to their room, her phone vibrated. She looked to see she had a message from Tate.

—Stay in your dresses. Jared and I will take you out when we finish here.

Anne showed the message to Sophia.

"Oh, wow, girl. I am glad I'm your friend. Did you see the muscles on his bodyguard pal? And speaking of texts—just how much have you two been conversing? I thought you were just spending extra time on the Lingo-mi app."

"I have been spending extra time on the app. I think it might be working."

Sophia slowly shook her head. "No redirecting. How much have you been texting?"

"Just a little every night. I was going to tell him about singing on Wednesday night, but the conversation took a different turn, and then it didn't come up last night." Anne kicked off her shoes and settled into the chair nearest the television. "I should message my family."

"Have you told them about Tate?" Sophia settled into the opposite chair.

"I don't generally tell people about acquaintances from junior high I run into in airports."

"Even if you are texting them every night?"

"You spend quite a bit of time messaging. Do you tell your family about it?"

"I'm just texting Briar. He got dumped again."

Anne took the opening. "What is this—the fourth time? When is he going to wake up and see he always runs to you?"

"He doesn't always run to me."

"Yes, he does. Face it. You are his Häagen-dazs." They'd met Briar their junior year of high school. Not once had he asked Sophia out, although they talked more than some couples she knew.

"You are comparing me to ice cream?"

Anne's phone buzzed, saving her from answering. "They are downstairs." She slipped on her shoes and smoothed her dress.

"You look awesome. Let's go." Sophia opened the door.

Anne took a deep breath. *I've got this.*

Sophia emerged first and said something to the uniformed guard. Anne followed, and his heart tapped harder in his chest. He wished Jared and Sophia could go do their own thing, but Mitch would kill them both. He sat with the driver, not thrilled with the change in plans. Not surprising, as he always groused when he didn't have enough time to check out a new location. Even Jared pointed out that the risk was no more than to any other American foursome out for dinner. The worst that could happen to them was the restaurant attempting to charge them twice the regular bill.

Jared held open the door to the six-seat luxury SUV Tate had rented in anticipation for tomorrow's trip to the Terracotta Army.

Tate took the back seat and assisted Anne into the spot beside him. "There is a fountain and music show at the Giant Wild Goose Pagoda that is supposed to be amazing. It's also one of the few things we found to do on short notice that didn't involve sitting at a bar."

Sophia turned in the middle seat. "I read about that. Isn't it part of the Daci'en Temple complex? I had that down for one of our weekend trips." The driver moved them into traffic, and Sophia turned back to the front. Jared engaged her in a conversation.

Tate turned to Anne. "Thanks for coming tonight. And, for the record, I didn't realize the orphanage and school you taught at had any connection, or I would have told you."

"Why were you there, anyway?"

"Searching for worthy charities. Awhile ago, I read that a few of the orphanages in China are struggling, so I thought I'd see what I could do to help."

"Does choosing a Chinese orphanage have anything to do with me?"

"You mean because you were adopted from China?"

Anne nodded. In the dim lighting, he couldn't tell if she was blushing.

"Perhaps in some way. I thought of you and your presentation when I read the article. I have charities in other places, too. This would be my first orphanage." Tate didn't disclose that he always donated 10 percent of his earnings to worthy causes. In the last year, he'd significantly increased his donations to causes that not only claimed to need his money but showed they could use it well.

"You remember my presentation?"

"Of course I do. Which is why I questioned the director about his inference that you were a product of his orphanage. Did you catch that part of his introduction?"

"No, I only understood *orphan*, *adopted*, *success*, and a few little words. Sophia explained the rest. Our supervisor was very upset that she didn't know I knew you because she thinks I ruined the orphanage's chances to get money."

"I haven't decided yet on this one. The director's quick lies and muddy finances give me pause. If I choose other institutions over this one, my choice will have had nothing to do with you. In the week you have been here, have you noticed anything about the children from the orphanage that would raise questions?"

Anne looked out the window for a moment. "No, they all seem healthy and maybe even happier than the residential students who live away from their families all week or even all year."

"I don't think I could do that to our—I mean my children. Put them in a residential school." Warmth flooded Tate's neck and face as he stumbled over his words.

Anne studied him for a long moment, then scooted over as far as the seat belt would allowed toward the center of the seat and spoke in a low tone. "Tate, I don't want to hurt you, but you don't really know me. I don't mind getting to know you better, but you need to know there isn't an 'us' or 'we' or 'our' in my vocabulary yet."

Tate nodded as she scooted back toward the window. "I understand. I didn't mean to make you feel uncomfortable." *Or say "our children."*

She moved her hand as if she were going to tuck a lock of hair behind her ear but dropped it back onto her lap after her fingers skimmed the edge of her updo. She looked at Sophia and Jared, who were discussing Japanese versus Chinese cuisine. "You have been thinking about me for years, and I have been trying not to think about you at all. Give me time to adjust to us being friends and you being a great person."

"As opposed to a not-great person?"

"You haven't been on my top-ten list for a very long time. But you are changing my perception."

Tate grinned and changed the subject to the crowded streets and various structures they passed. The driver found a place to drop them off, and they wound their way to the entrance, where Jared paid the ticket fee.

Sophia looked around. "I think we are overdressed."

"It's dark. Who is going to notice?" Anne's heel caught in a sidewalk crack.

Tate offered her his arm. "I'd feel bad if you twisted an ankle." They followed the rest of the crowd to the viewing area, Mitch a few paces behind them. Jared led them to an empty bench with a good view of the area.

The coolness of the cement bench leaked through the fabric of Tate's pants. "Would you like to sit on my jacket?"

Anne touched the sleeve of the suit coat. "Armani?"

"I think so."

She shook her head. "I would be too worried about ruining it. The bench isn't that cold."

The lights dimmed, and the fountains ebbed and flowed to the music. Higher and higher, faster and faster, the water rose to the sky as the music intensified. Light danced through the droplets. The audience clapped and shouted. Tate glanced down at Anne as she clapped. Her face was as relaxed and open as it had been in the middle of her song tonight. He turned back to the show before she could catch him studying her. After his faux pas on the way over, he needed to back off. He decided courtship was more difficult than negotiating a contract with a Chinese tech firm.

The music crescendoed, and the finale played. Tate joined the others in their cheers. Once the music died and the colored lights faded, the park lights came back on, illuminating the walkways.

"That was amazing. So much better than what I saw online." Anne stood before he could do the chivalrous thing and help her up. They waited for the crowd to clear. Mitch appeared to look at his watch, then nodded to Jared, a signal it was time to move out.

Anne took Tate's arm again. They walked back to the parking lot in silence. It was enough to have her at his side. He wouldn't ask for more—yet.

Soy milk and youtiao—the fried, churro-type pastry was not Anne's favorite breakfast, mostly because it reminded her of her great-grandma Williams's milk toast. There was something wrong about soaking the fried flour stick in milk until it was soft, even if the resulting sweet flavor was more dessert-ish than breakfast-y. This morning she was too impatient to wait for it to soften. Sophia didn't even bother and consumed them separately. They ran back up to their room and finished getting ready.

"You never told me how often you two have been texting." Sophia wound her ponytail into a messy bun.

"Maybe it's because I am avoiding the subject. Once I answer that, you are going to ask me all sorts of questions I am not ready for."

"How do you know that?"

Anne paused mid toothpaste squeeze. "Seriously? After twelve years of friendship, how could I not? But to keep you from pestering me, Tate wants to see if our friendship could go someplace. And considering that just last week he was on my 'people I wish I'd never met' list, I am not ready. I think he has this romanticized view of me that isn't me." She stuffed the toothbrush into her mouth.

Sophia stopped applying her lip gloss. "Tate Gilman. The billionaire Tate Gilman, who, according to you, went from not toofhot, wants to date you, and you don't think he is interested? Are you insane?"

"Mm-mm-mm."

"Don't give me that I-don't-know mumble mess. Is there any chemistry?"

Anne gave special attention to her back molars to avoid answering. They hadn't really touched. Her arm on his jacket. Their shoulders bumped a few times. Looking at him did make her heart speed up, but then, what breathing woman's wouldn't? She moved to her incisors and shrugged.

Sophia put her lip gloss away. "You are going to keep brushing to avoid answering, aren't you?" She left their little bathroom.

Anne's phone beeped as she spit out her toothpaste.

"Is that them?" Sophia rechecked her cross-body bag.

"Yes, they are about a block away." Anne grabbed her bag and hurried out of the room before Sophia could ask another question.

The seating arrangements were the same as yesterday. From a guidebook, Sophia read the history of the terracotta statues. "I guess it is better than burying the real soldiers. But I can't believe they employed so many people just to prepare for a burial. I mean, really, 'Hi, thirteen-year-old emperor. Time to prepare to die.' How morbid is that?"

No one answered, or needed to, as Sophia continued reading from the guidebook.

Next to Anne in the space between their seats lay Tate's hand. An invitation or a dare, Anne couldn't tell. Perhaps he just liked to rest his hand that way, palm up. His hand looked strong, not soft like he never worked, but there were no noticeable calluses. Perhaps there would be if she touched it. His arm looked solid too. It had been last night. If she just reached out to touch it, she would know if there was a spark. But if he was just resting it there, it would be too weird to reach out and grab it. And if there were no sparks…Anne looked up from Tate's hand to find his gray-blue eyes watching her. He moved his hand back to his lap, his lips quirking up in a half smile. Anne turned her attention to the scene outside the window and hoped he couldn't tell she was blushing.

Beyond her window, the faces of strangers who looked like her, but not, passed by on their way to shop or to work. Aside from what she'd learned from documentaries and blog posts, Anne understood little about their lives. The thought that some of these people could be her relatives bounced around her head. How could she be related to people she shared so little in common with?

The talking in the car ceased. Anne turned from the window to find Sophia, Jared, and Tate all looking at her. "What?"

"Jared asked how long you've been singing. I couldn't remember." Sophia sat sideways in her seat.

"I've always sung. That is how Mother said she got me to learn English. I didn't want to speak at first. When she gave me music, I practiced. I think I had all the Disney songs down before I was five."

Jared gave her a smile. "I've had the song you sang in my mind since last night. Have you ever sung on stage?"

"Not really." Anne looked at Sophia, hoping she wouldn't spill about the audition for Sing4Life. "I sang in the college choir and had a few solos."

"I remember you singing when we were in school. You were so much better than the rest of us." The intensity in Tate's eyes forced her to look away.

"Ironic, isn't it? I learned English by singing, but I couldn't seem to learn Chinese the same way." Anne focused on Sophia as she spoke.

Tate asked his next question in Mandarin. "Has your understanding improved this week?"

"*Shì.*" Anne hoped she'd pronounced the word for "yes" correctly.

"Wow! His app worked. I didn't think you would know what he was asking." Sophia's vote of confidence was not very encouraging.

"Did you enjoy it?" Tate spoke in Mandarin again.

"It wasn't as *nán* as I thought it would be." Anne held her fingers a half inch apart. "Even a little bit fun."

"Can you say that in Mandarin?" asked Tate.

"*Xiao Xiao de leu.*" Her statement sounded more like a question.

"'Small fun.' That is pretty good." Tate gave her a smile that made her want to try harder. If he had looked half as handsome in the seventh grade, she might have tried harder to learn Chinese then.

The vehicle slowed. Mitch turned in the front seat. "Do me a favor. Stay together. I'm concerned about tourists recognizing Tate. Ladies, it wasn't my intention, but having you along is a good cover for Tate. He is so rarely seen with a date, I hope it will keep even his most ardent fans from recognizing him. Miss Williams, I hate to ask you this, but will you act more like a girlfriend? You know, hold hands and that sort of thing. Miss Clyde, just be a friend. Jared may need to move, so no hand-holding for you." Mitch ended his request with a chuckle as the driver parked.

Tate set his hand back on the seat, palm up. "You don't need to if you don't want, but I promise I won't bite."

Anne bit her lip. At least she knew he was offering this time. She lay her hand on top of his. The warmth of his palm traveled up her arm like the heat of the flame of a Bunsen burner. Tate interlaced his fingers with hers, igniting an unexpected chemical reaction and setting her heart spinning.

Yes, they had chemistry.

"The photos don't do the warriors justice." It was the only coherent thought Tate could form while holding Anne's hand. When Mitch had suggested Anne pretend to be his girlfriend, Tate had been tempted to fire him. However, after an hour of escorting Anne around the exhibits, he wondered if a raise might be in order. They passed a few other American tourists, but no one looked his way. As Anne leaned into him and pointed to a detail on one of the chariots, Tate inhaled her scent—something light and flowery he couldn't define. She asked a question, and he nodded.

Anne gave him a sharp look. "Are you serious?"

Tate shook his head and hoped his subconscious mind could figure out what he'd missed.

"That's a relief. For a moment, I was worried all the money had gone to your head."

They moved on to the next display. Behind him, Jared and Sophia laughed. The uneasy feeling that the humor was at his expense filled him. Tate turned, and Jared looked away, the laughter stopping. The constant watching of bodyguards and associations was one reason he had dated little since his app had taken off, never mind that his social life was nonexistent pre-app. To be alone with a woman, he needed to have her in a safe space, which left his place, and inviting a woman in on the first, or even tenth, date wasn't his style. Until this moment, the constant presence of chaperones had never bothered him. It helped most women keep their distance. How was he supposed to have a private conversation with Anne in a country where no place was considered safe by his security team?

Anne touched his arm. "What is wrong?"

"Nothing."

"Then why are you frowning?"

And this was why he didn't play poker and why he practiced his presentations. "I was thinking through a problem I can't solve. Sorry, I shouldn't have gotten distracted." He rubbed his thumb along the top of hers.

Anne's eyes widened. "Is there something I can help you with?"

Tate leaned closer so he could whisper. "I'm trying to figure out how to date you with the obstacles associated with my bodyguards and a country that thrives on surveillance."

"Oh." Anne's blush earned him a sharp look from Sophia.

They walked around a magnificent terracotta horse, Tate moving them several yards away from Jared and Sophia. Mitch observed from a dozen paces away.

Anne gave his hand the slightest tug. "We'll have to wait until we are both back home."

"I can't do things like this in the US. Too many people—"

Five feet away, a woman screeched, "It's Tate Gilman!"

Tate pretended not to notice and turned his back to the distraction. He spoke to Anne in Mandarin. "Speak only Chinese."

Two women, who, judging by their blonde hair and UCLA T-shirts were American college students, shoved past the three or four people between them. "I told you, Cin. You're Tate, aren't you?"

Tate replied in a well-practiced Scandinavian accent. "Sorry, miss. You have me confused with an old friend?"

The taller woman shook her head. "Nice try. I read about that Swedish act in a blog." She turned to Anne and spoke slowly. "Do you"—she pointed at Anne, then at her head—"know your boyfriend is famous and rich?" She pointed to Tate and rubbed her fingers together.

Anne furrowed her brow and turned to Tate. "*Zhùmíng*?"

Tate answered in Mandarin, gauging the reaction of both women. "The crazy American thinks I am a rich and famous person named Tate Gilman. The bleach must have killed her brain cells." Around him, a couple of Chinese smiled and turned away, but neither woman even frowned.

Anne nodded and turned to the blondes. "Crazy bimbo, he poor. Me pay ticket. Go, go. He my man." She stepped into the blonde's space and waved her hand in a shooing motion, then added in perfect Mandarin, "Crazy American."

Jared and Sophia reached their side as the two blondes walked off. "Well done." Sophia commented in Mandarin.

"Lucky for me, people see what they expect to see. I couldn't have done that for long." Anne's voice was barely louder than a whisper.

Jared herded the group to a place near a vacant wall. "Well played, Anne. Mitch isn't very happy right now. His stay-together warning was for you not to ditch me, Tate."

They continued through the exhibits without further incident. As they made the walk back to the parking lot, Anne slowed. "Is it always like that in public?"

"Depends where I am. I am not a household name to most Chinese, so I have a small detail here. Some places in the US, I have four to six bodyguards. The *1984* Big Brother issues here give me a little freedom from being mobbed by the locals. At the same time, even the birds make it hard to know when I am being watched."

Anne studied the sky. "I heard about the dove drones. That is almost too weird to believe. Like a young-adult postapocalyptic novel."

"Now you know the problem I've been contemplating. We will not get much alone time while I'm here. I fly back tomorrow."

"Did the contract get approved?"

"No, it's in limbo again. I think stalling is part of the Chinese strategy. Part of me wants to forget it, but I think I should keep trying for a while."

They reached the SUV. Tate helped Anne in and followed. Mitch and the driver discussed where to go for lunch and for the promised ice cream. Sophia leaned into the seat and closed her eyes. "I'm exhausted. I haven't walked so much since we got here. Or even weeks before we arrived."

The driver pulled out of the lot, the only sounds in the car coming from the stereo system.

Anne reached over and took Tate's hand. He used his free hand to trace her knuckles. He didn't speak. She was holding his hand when there was no reason to pretend. He wasn't waiting eleven weeks. He would find a way they could have a few private moments together.

True to his word, Tate gave Anne the opportunity to order the ice cream, which he paid for. Anne got all the orders correct, or perhaps the older gentleman behind the counter had understood from her pointing. Either way, including the translation at the museums, Anne had spoken more Mandarin in one day than she had in her last week of the immersion program. She might have to give Tate more credit for the app's success than she'd planned.

"We probably should eat a more traditional dessert." Sophia stuck her spoon in her bowl again.

"The Chinese are credited with the creation of one of the earliest recipes for ice cream that involved milk." Anne took a bite of her plain chocolate ice cream. She would have ordered some add-ins, but she had no idea of the words she wanted to use. She suspected the others had simplified their own orders to help her.

Tate finished his bowl of vanilla. "Marco Polo reportedly brought back a recipe for a sorbet of sorts from China."

"And here I thought ice cream was American." Jared finished his chocolate.

"I wrote a research report on ice cream in high school. The first ice cream mentioned in America was in 1777 served at some dinner hosted by a governor. It makes sense they had it before then," said Tate.

"Is there a subject you didn't write a report on?" Jared shook his head. "I think you wrote reports just for the fun of it."

Anne sat back in her seat. "You wrote extra reports when we had class together. I remember Chen Lǎoshī limiting you to one per assignment."

Tate's neck reddened as the rest of them laughed. "If we are done, maybe we should go see the city wall since I booked us a bike tour that starts in an hour."

Sophia clapped her hands. "You are working on all my big tourist attractions for the city."

The guided tour of the wall didn't leave much time for talking as they dodged tourists and cyclists. Whenever they stopped for the tour guide to tell them about the buildings they were passing, Tate held her hand. Occasionally he would run his thumb down the side of hers, sending a distracting tingle up her arm. She ignored the disapproving glare of the guide as she listened to the history of the area and studied the rooftops of the ancient buildings.

As the sun set, the top of the wall emptied of tourists. They returned their bikes and thanked the guide, who took Anne's helmet and spoke sharply in Chinese. She understood enough to be offended but wasn't clear as to why.

Tate responded to the guide in English. "You are confused. She is just as American as I am. And if anyone is trying to trap someone into a marriage with a rich American, it's me trapping her."

The guide's eyes grew wide, and he muttered several apologies in both English and Chinese before leaving them.

"I can't believe he said that." Sophia shook her head.

"I would congratulate Tate on his app, because I thought I understood more ...however, I think I am glad I caught less than half of what he said." Anne hoped she sounded cheerful.

Tate turned to Mitch. "Give me ten?"

"Five." Mitch nodded to a section of the wall where no one stood between the red lanterns.

Tate waited to speak until they were as far from the rest of the group as Mitch indicated they could go. "I hope I didn't embarrass you."

"No. He called me a prostitute, didn't he?"

"More or less." Tate reddened.

"From your blush, I will assume it was more and be glad I didn't understand it all. Thanks for defending me."

Tate took her other hand in his. "I wish I could have been more eloquent about it."

Anne looked him in the eye. "I thought it was well-spoken. *Are* you trying to trap me?"

"Not trap. More like offer you cookies so you'll come over to the dark side. I'd offer kisses, but we have too many chaperones."

Anne's cheeks flooded with warmth.

Tate released one of her hands and tucked a lock of hair behind her ear. "I don't think a first kiss should be experienced with an audience."

Anne closed her eyes and leaned into his palm where it rested against her head. After a few moments, she opened her eyes. "I think this is good for now." She stepped back, or tried to, but the wall blocked her.

Tate dropped his hand. "I still wish we could talk without worrying about eavesdroppers."

"I could invite you back to my place if you don't get the wrong idea."

He laughed. "Even if we could get Sophia to be someplace else, I guarantee your apartment is bugged."

"How do you know? It's not like Sophia and I discuss anything interesting."

"I don't. But I'll bet you a date at the Great Wall that if you complain about being cold tonight, in the morning someone will offer you extra blankets."

"If I lose, how does that work?"

"Either way, we go to the Great Wall. You just buy my ticket if you lose."

"I think I will lose."

Mitch approached. "Sorry. Time's up. I have confirmed our dinner reservations."

Tate took her hand and walked over to where Jared and Sophia were talking. "What are you two lollygagging about for? We have a dinner waiting for us."

Anne held on to his hand as they descended the stairway. She wished the day didn't have to end.

Back in the SUV after dinner, Anne reached for his hand again. Tate debated about sliding over to the center seat. Jared would notice, and there was something about holding her hand when the others weren't watching that made it special. "What did you guys think of those English translations on the menu?"

Sophia turned around in her seat. "My favorite was 'homemade skin frozen.'"

Jared laughed. "No, 'rotten garlic intestine,' wins."

"I don't understand why no one tried the 'fried enema,'" said Mitch.

"I think this is why they need Lingo-mi," said Tate.

"Says the man who ordered 'riches and honor your elbow.' I thought my language was bad, but I did enjoy the 'private and refreshing side dish,'" said Anne.

"My 'mixes gross with sweet-and-sour sauce' was definitely misnamed. The sweet-and-sour sauce made the dish." Sophia turned back to the front.

Too soon the driver pulled into a spot near the school.

"Is there a school function tonight?" asked Mitch.

Sophia shook her head. "Not that they told us. But the street seems crowded, doesn't it?"

"Jared, come check it out with me. Sophia, I doubt it is dangerous, but will you see if you can access the dorm?"

The three of them exited the SUV.

Anne turned to Tate, her brow creased. "Does Mitch do that often?"

"Whenever he doesn't like a situation. Better to leave me in the getaway car, so to speak." He raised her fingers to his lips. The driver was watching them, and there probably wasn't enough time to do a kiss justice. "Can I see your phone?"

Anne handed it over.

"Open it, please?"

"What are you going to do?"

"I want to see if I can get a more secure texting app on your phone. I fly out in the morning, and I want to keep talking to you." Tate opened his phone. Anne's phone lacked the necessary technology to allow him to drop the beta copy of his secure texting program onto it. Tate handed the phone back. "Sorry. When I come back in two weeks, I'll bring you a card or something so we can talk about anything."

Anne shuddered. "Kind of creepy, isn't it?"

The side door flew open, and Jared stuck his head in. "Anne, I'll walk you to your door. Mitch doesn't want Tate in the crowd as he heard people saying his name."

He gave Anne's fingertips a squeeze, and she was gone.

Jared returned to the SUV with Mitch. "Not sure what that was. But your name was mentioned as we passed the guards."

The driver took them back to their luxury hotel.

As soon as he was alone in his room, he texted Anne. **Sorry I didn't get to walk you to the door.**

— I understand. You didn't lose any dating points.

There are dating points?

— Super-secret woman thing. Just kidding.

Good. I would hate to have to figure out a way to get extra credit.
— As a teacher, I don't believe in extra credit.
How do your students survive?
— They are second graders. Citizenship grades count.
Oh, I was rude to a man today and lied to a couple California girls.
— I know. That is why you have an A in citizenship. :)
So you are not dumping me yet?
—Nope.
Whew. Thanks. I should go pack.
—Sleep well and have a good flight.
Good night to you too.

There was an email message from his lawyer. They were still stuck on the wording of a few paragraphs. *Good!* Business would allow him to come back to China without raising any eyebrows. It would be easier to see Anne in a different city. How would she react to flying to Beijing for the weekend? With Sophia, of course.

Jared knocked on the door. "Mitch is wondering if he needs to build Anne into your plans for when we come back in two weeks."

"I hope so."

"I still can't believe you found her after all these years and that she likes you." Jared shook his head.

"I'm starting to believe in fairy tales myself. I wish I'd found her before all the money. I feel like there will be no way to find a private moment."

"Once she is stateside it will be easier to coordinate. At least her roommate is willing to go along, even if she isn't into me. Which is the way it needs to be if I'm to do my job of watching your back."

"My life cuts into your social life, too, doesn't it?" Tate tossed his shirts into the suitcase.

"I knew what I was signing up for. My question is, do you?"

"With Anne?" Tate paused. "No idea. Isn't that great?"

Jared shook his head and left the room muttering something about addlepated lovers.

Tate smiled. He enjoyed being addlepated.

The flight back from Beijing qualified as one of the most disorienting flights in the world. After over fifteen hours on a plane, his phone shouldn't be telling him he'd arrived two hours before he left. Jared and Mitch looked just as disoriented standing in the customs line.

"Do you have anything to declare?"

I left my heart in China. "No." Tate had purchased more souvenirs than he ever had on his earlier trips.

A fresh team of bodyguards met them at the exit, keeping anyone who recognized his fatigued body from getting too near. One nice thing about bodyguards was he didn't have to worry about freeway traffic or being too fatigued to drive.

The house was clean, with not a soul inside. When his housekeeper would be in again, Tate had no idea. Today was still Sunday, only Anne was probably getting ready for work on Monday. He checked the world clock on his phone. No, it was the middle of the night in Xi'an.

Anne had left a message hoping he had a good flight.

Landed safely. I am still in Sunday. I guess that happens when you have a fifteen-hour time difference and a fifteen-hour flight. If I don't answer when you text, I'm asleep.

And dreaming of you.

The children didn't behave like it was a Monday that killed the weekend. Anne had no difficulty getting the six-year-olds' attention as they sang the alphabet song. She changed to a clapping song where the children took turns deciding what word started with the letter.

"A is for . . . aardvark."

"B is for . . . banana."

The children giggled as they moved on to animals.

"Lion."

"Mongoose."

"Narwhal."

Who had taught them that? Anne exchanged a look with Sophia, who bit her lip.

"Yak!"

"Zebra!"

Sophia started her section of conversational phrases. They'd learned last week not to ask the children about their weekend as they all had the same weekend—one hazard of living at a residential school. If one child visited the zoo, they all experienced the zoo. Only one or two children went home each weekend. With the uniforms, it was hard to tell economic differences between children; however, Anne guessed that the children who went home were from the wealthiest families, as were the preschoolers who returned home nightly.

Their lesson hour ended all too soon, and the regular teacher started the children on their hourly stretches and eye exercises. Sophia followed along with the exercises, counting to eight while rubbing her eyes.

Anne gathered her belongings. Last week she learned that after each teaching unit, the children cleaned the classroom. They slid the desks to the wall and threw a bucketful of water in the center of the cement floor and swished it around. By the last class of the day, sitting on the floor wasn't an option as after several washings the concrete never quite dried. In the summer it wasn't too bad. In the winter it could be miserable.

As the children pushed the desks back, Anne and Sophia made their escape for the fourth-grade classroom.

The fourth graders had progressed to writing and had each written a short essay. Today they presented the papers they'd written last week on their favorite foods. It was obvious they'd helped one another in their work. It was one difference with the collective mindset the children had. All of them needed to succeed. So the brighter students constantly helped and tutored the slower. Other than gently correcting mispronunciations and grammar, there wasn't much for Anne and Sophia to do. Ultimately, their teacher, who spoke superb English, would deliver the grades or marks he used.

Anne and Sophia ate lunch at one end of the play yard, their noodles and vegetables served on recyclable trays. A few of the students came over as they finished to ask them questions.

"What do you eat for lunch in America?"

"Why don't American cartoons have speaking?" This from a young boy who had watched Roadrunner cartoons over the weekend.

"Will you sing a song for us?"

Anne hadn't expected that question.

"Disney," mouthed Sophia.

That should be safe. After all, the music was in the music room. As Anne found a starting note and started into one of the famous princess songs, more children gathered around. Anne gestured for them to join her, but none did. Kim Lǎoshī stood behind them with her arms crossed. When the song ended, the other teachers ushered the children back into the building.

"Don't sing that song again." Kim Lǎoshī frowned.

"Sorry, I thought it was one from the music room." Anne stood so that Kim Lǎoshī couldn't look down at her.

"Yes, but some words are different. We changed them. Too western."

"My apologies."

"You should not sing at all for them or they will ask you to sing every day and we will not have order. Sing only in the music room. What do you have next?"

Sophia stood, her empty lunch tray in hand. "We have three music classes."

"Make sure you teach them the words in the book." Kim Lǎoshī left them.

Anne picked up her garbage. "Will I ever do anything she approves of?"

"Kim Lǎoshī wishes she sang like you." Sophia added her paper tray to the bin.

"You say that about everyone."

"Because it's true. Either that or she wishes she could date Tate."

"I doubt she knows who he is." Anne turned on the light in the music room.

"After Friday night she does, and she knows everything her search engine finds about him."

"Then she doesn't know much." Anne had looked online last week, finding only the barest of outlines about Tate, mostly talking about the Lingo-mi app and displaying a few photos. There was no mention of the number of languages his app taught or his lack of a college degree. There was no mention of his family or personal life.

"Other than he is a fine specimen of a man and richer than King Midas." Several students walked into the room, ending the conversation.

They started class by singing the national anthem, "March of the Volunteers," in Mandarin, then English.

Arise, ye who refuse to be slaves!
With our flesh and blood, let us build a new Great Wall!
As China faces its greatest peril
From each one the urgent call to action comes forth.
Arise! Arise! Arise!
Millions of but one heart
Braving the enemies' fire! March on!
Braving the enemies' fire! March on!
March on! March, march on!

Anne liked the sound of the song in Mandarin, at least before she understood the words. The more she pondered the lyrics, the more they bothered her. Her natural mother and father and perhaps a brother and his wife sang this song. Did they believe they were in peril from people like her?

Anne moved on to the next song, a ballad from a popular Australian band. None of the words had been modified, making it easy for Anne to ponder more on her previous thought.

Who, exactly, were people like her? She wished she could talk to Tate, but the thoughts could be considered political, and if the app were monitored...It would wait until he was back, or maybe she'd forget it entirely.

—Good Morning from tomorrow! Tate read Anne's message sent hours ago. He did the math and realized she'd sent it after midnight her time. The clock on his nightstand declared dinner was over on the West Coast. The rumble in his stomach concurred.

Good evening from yesterday. How is tomorrow going? Tate didn't wait for an answer. She was probably teaching. It would take them a day or two to find a time to converse.

In the kitchen he found a half lasagna the housekeeper left to be heated, along with salad and a note about the bread in the freezer. He dished up a plate and put it in the microwave, then read the message again. **If you are in tomorrow while I am in today, does that make you my future?** As a pickup line it would never work, but phone flirting? He hit send.

Grabbing his laptop, he sat down to eat dinner and catch up on what he'd missed the last week and a half. Fortunately, his team kept him up on all matters business through their secure phones and apps. One thing he'd learned early on when forming his company was to hire competent people and stand clear while they did their job.

His phone beeped.

— Only if you are my past.

I guess we better stay in the present. Are you teaching?

— Class break. I have fifteen minutes. Did you sleep on your flight?

Not much. Did you get lost today?

— Not a fair question. Good thing I team teach, or I would have walked into the high school classes and taught them animal names.

You might have noticed they were taller than you.

—Ha, ha. I'm not that short.

They spent the remainder of the fifteen minutes chatting about nothing significant. The emojis on the chat app didn't express enough emotions, but Tate used them to make sure she knew when he was joking.

— Gotta go. I'll write later.

He wished he dared call her. But he suspected the Chinese government might be too interested in what he had to say. Some called him paranoid. He was. The app had a long-enough lag he assumed any conversations about politics or religion would be flagged. How was he supposed to talk about meaningful things? Could he get her to understand his heart enough in texts? Cyrano de Bergerac had gotten a woman to fall in love with him, or rather, his friend, through letters. It was worth a try.

Tate created a new email account through a free service and started to write.

Anne,

Our texting wasn't enough tonight. There are things I want to share, and I want to get to know you better, but mini paragraphs are not enough.

Tate stared at the blinking cursor and had no idea what to write next. He'd talked of his grandfather and told her how he'd thought she was cute in the seventh grade. Some verbose letter detailing her virtues would scare her off. It would scare him off. And he didn't dare write about work. The Chinese didn't need to know his thoughts on that score. How stupid! He wanted to talk and share but had nothing to share. How did couples get to know each other? No wonder distance relationships didn't work well.

He loaded his dirty dish in the dishwasher. Not ready to go back to bed, he turned on video streaming. Instead of choosing the latest live-action comic-book movie, he scrolled through the backlist of Hearthfire movies, looking for one based on a long-distance relationship. He needed ideas and wasn't beneath getting them from a chick flick. There weren't any.

He pulled up a search engine on his phone. It was less than helpful as almost every suggestion for long distance relationships included a helpful amount of video chat. Then he found an idea that worked—have a hobby together. A game they could play online? What games could be played across the Great Cyber

Wall? Another site talked about watching a movie together. That could work. He opened the email.

> **Do you play any online games—other than my language app? I'm trying to find something we can do together. Another suggestion is watching a movie together. Do you have a show downloaded to your phone or access to a movie you want to watch? We can start it at the same time, then comment. Not as fun, but we could pretend …**

The whole point of watching a movie with a date was so you could hold hands or snuggle. It was a dumb idea, but with the complications of an unsecure line, it was at least an idea.

> **I can get up two hours early if you can stay up an hour late.**
>
> **Can't wait to see you again.**
>
> **B**

Only when he went to hit send did he realize he didn't have Anne's email address. He retyped the email into four texts and sent them.

> **— I only have this old movie on my phone. Long story. I'll see what I can find. We could watch it my Saturday night/your early Saturday morning. Sophia will probably end up watching with me. I only have solitaire on my phone. They sound like fine ideas. Later.**

Tate read the message twice. Cool. He had his first long-distance date.

"Williams Anne and Clyde Sophia, please come with me." Kim Lǎoshī waited in the hallway outside of the second-grade classroom. She led them upstairs to the administrative offices where the director of the orphanage, the woman who was the equivalent of a principal, and a man Anne didn't recognize stood in a small room.

"We will make this brief." The principal spoke in such heavily accented English that *brief* sounded more like *reef*. "Your deception has cost the orphanage much money. You are dismissed."

"Dismissed?" Anne and Sophia asked in unison.

The orphanage director spoke in Mandarin. Kim Lǎoshī translated. "You didn't say Gilman Tate was your boyfriend. Now he says he will not donate to our orphanage."

"He is just a friend." At least he had been five days ago. Their time together last weekend and the texts they'd shared constituted a little more than friendship, but it was too early to call him a boyfriend.

Sophia saved Anne from protesting further. "What do you mean dismissed? As in you don't want us in the room or fired from a job?"

"They mean fired from this position. We will contact company to tell them you broke contract by lying."

"Lying about what?" Anne had been accused of many things in her life, but dishonesty wasn't one of them. Well, other than the time she'd broken Mom's vase, but she was seven.

"I asked you on the tour of the building if you had American boyfriends." Kim Lǎoshī folded her arms.

"And I told you I didn't." Anne couldn't wrap her mind around it. They were both getting fired because of her knowing Tate.

"But you were seen at Terracotta Army and on city wall holding hands. You even said he was your boyfriend to American blonde woman." The businessman held an uncanny knowledge of their Saturday.

Sophia's face turned red. "So you are firing us because Anne held Tate's hand?"

"No, because she lied. If she had told that Gilliam Tate was American boyfriend, then Williams Anne would not sing, and director would not be accused of lying."

It was the money.

"I didn't realize I was obligated to disclose a list of all the people I have ever known. I did not lie when Kim Lǎoshī asked me about American boyfriend. There wasn't one. But sometimes things change. I didn't know Tate was going to be here. You did not tell me, nor did he. I am not responsible for what the director said in his introduction. If you had asked me about my journey from China to America, I would have said I was born in Lanzhou."

The principal stepped forward. "You must leave school. Guards watch you pack."

"Where are we supposed to go?" demanded Sophia.

"Not my problem." The principal nodded to the door, where two guards stood. "Be gone in half hour, or we will call police."

Anne left the room first. Sophia grabbed her arm before she turned down the wrong hallway. Neither spoke as they returned to the dorm, followed by the guards and Kim Lǎoshī. As soon as they opened their bedroom door, Kim Lǎoshī held out her hand. "Keys. You will not need them again." Anne pulled out her suitcase. Instead of packing with the precision of a Tetris master, she started at one end of the closet, more concerned that she might leave something in the rush of things. She rolled her dirty clothes into a plastic bag to keep them separate. Other than a souvenir fan, the only thing Anne had purchased in Xi'an was the black dress, so everything fit easily back in her case. Sophia pulled out a collapsible bag and filled it with her extra purchases, including a terracotta warrior replica.

Anne went into the bathroom and shut the door. Immediately there was a knock. Anne opened the door to Kim Lǎoshī. "Keep the door open."

"But I need to—" *have a moment alone.*

Kim Lǎoshī shook her head. "Then keep the door open."

"Why? I will not steal the toilet paper." They already had stuffed half rolls in their bags. Most public toilets didn't have paper in the stalls.

Kim Lǎoshī only crossed her arms and looked at Anne's phone clutched in her hand.

Anne understood. They weren't worried about her taking anything as much as they were her using her phone. She gathered her toiletries and returned to her suitcase. One guard opened the cupboard and refrigerator and pulled out a box of cookies and leftover food and set them on the table. Anne scooped up the cookies but left the remains of last night's dinner.

Sophia zipped up her suitcase. "I think it is time for Elvis to leave the building."

The guards and Kim Lǎoshī followed them to the street. The guards went back and stood at the door, but Kim Lǎoshī followed them several feet to the corner. "I suggest you take the night train to Beijing. I don't know what your company will do when the principal calls."

"You mean they haven't told them?" Sophia adjusted her backpack.

Kim Lǎoshī shrugged and left.

Sophia tugged at her luggage handle. "Let's head to the north subway station. We can put our bags in a locker and enjoy the rest of the day. I'm not ready to leave Xi'an. I still wanted to get some calligraphy rubbings."

"We need to find Wi-Fi so we can contact the head office in Beijing. They may want us to do something else."

"I'll call them." Sophia pulled out her phone. She spoke first in Mandarin, then in English, as she described what happened, then she hung up. "They will call us back. Congratulations. You are the only person they have ever had lose her job over an American boyfriend. They kept asking me if you had behaved inappropriately."

Anne felt her face grow warm. She had nothing to be embarrassed about. "Should we still go to the train station?"

"Why not? At least we can put our bags there. Maybe they will put us in one of the other schools around here. I'd like more time in Xi'an."

The subway wasn't as full in the middle of the day as it was when they normally used it after work.

At the train station they rented three lockers to store their bags—one for Anne and two for Sophia.

Anne checked the train schedule. Until they heard from Beijing, it didn't matter too much. "Let's go to the market. Maybe I can find the souvenirs I want and we can find fun foods to try."

They passed a red-and-yellow food cart. Sophia stopped. "Do you think donkey meat tastes like horse? I had horse once in Spain."

The cart looked clean enough. Anne decided her day couldn't get worse. "I'll split one with you."

They found a vendor who sold the rubbings Sophia wanted as well as another one selling terracotta and bronzed warriors. Anne chose three of the small ones to take to her mother and sisters as well as two horses for her father and brother.

Sophia's phone rang. She showed Anne the Beijing number before answering in Mandarin. The conversation changed to English, and Sophia again related the cause of their dismissal. "No,

Anne didn't lie. She didn't have a boyfriend. Not that a boyfriend should have any relation to her employment, anyway."

Sophia nodded and listened, then handed the phone to Anne.

"Hello?"

"Miss Williams, this is Mr. Peters." The man spoke with a clipped British accent. "I have spoken to the administrators of the school and your roommate, and I am perplexed. Why do you think they let you go?"

"Other than that they didn't get a grant for the orphanage because it turned out their special visitor knew me? Not that they would say that."

"Were there any other problems at the school?"

"They seemed displeased to learn I was of Chinese birth. And I sang the full original lyrics to a song, not realizing the copy in the music room had been modified to better reflect Chinese culture." Anne rolled her eyes at Sophia.

"They mentioned you didn't look American as one of their complaints. I am not sure what to do with you two as the program is full for the summer and I don't want to play musical teachers. We do have a preschool here in Beijing that isn't staffed during the summer. That would give you a half day. Take the train back tonight and come to the office in the morning. Text us your arrival time. I am not sure what you'll be able to find on such short notice."

"Thank you, Mr. Peters. We will see you in the morning." Anne handed the phone back to Sophia. "Let's go see what tickets we can get. I don't want to have to buy a standing ticket if we are on a twelve-hour train ride."

"Ditto."

Tate reread Anne's text in disbelief.

—Long story short, they fired us. I'll tell you more later. The first text came in around 3:00 p.m. Xi'an time, which was around midnight on the West Coast. Tate had slept through the beep, as well as the one that followed it a few minutes later.

—Oh, only the school fired us. We are going back to Beijing to work elsewhere.

Another set of texts came in about a half hour later.

—If we can find a train.

—I don't want a standing-grade ticket and to spend twelve hours of my life leaning against a wall.

—Sorry for whining. Not the best day.

An hour later, Anne texted again.

—Sophia for the win. She got us two soft-sleeper tickets on the 19:21 train!!!

At four in the morning, another text came in with a selfie of Anne lying on the top bunk of a train compartment.

— I hope I don't fall off in my sleep. You would be too tall for this bed.

— Remember the blondes? They are the other two passengers in our compartment.

— They don't recognize me. :)

— Night!

That was only two hours ago. Maybe Anne would still be awake.
Good morning. How is the train?

No answer came immediately, so Tate went downstairs to his home gym. When he was in college, he enjoyed the competitive camaraderie of a public gym, but it was one of those things forever lost to him when his photo had popped up on the news. Most of his friends didn't mind when women followed them around during the workouts, but as his financial worth had increased, so had the brazenness of some women. It got to where he could hardly exercise, so he quit and built a home center. All the bodyguards who stayed on had access to his gym. Mostly because working out alone stunk.

Tate ran two miles before the next text came in.

—Not too bad. Rocking motion lulls me to sleep, but stops wake me up.

He grabbed his phone and took a seat in the sauna. **I have so many questions I want to ask. How are you?**

— I've had time for the shock to wear off. So I am mostly angry now. At least they didn't put us on the first flight to the USA.

How is Sophia?

— She is being nice about everything, since, essentially, they fired me and she was collateral damage.

What did you do?

— Failed to have ESP and see the future. Nothing I am going to text about. But I did nothing wrong. It's more one of those wrong people at the wrong time things. How was your yesterday?

There was no avoiding the change in subject. Tate told her a bit about business, keeping everything vague since they were using the Chinese app and he assumed he had no true privacy on it. When he'd sat in the sauna so long he thought he would evaporate, he headed for his room.

I should be back in Beijing late next week. Want to do something next Saturday?

— Sophia and I were going to spend the day at the Great Wall. First thing on my China bucket list. Even if you can't see it from space.

You believed that rumor?

—Yup. In seventh grade, this geeky kid gave a presentation on it. He said you could see it from space. He had maps and everything.

Oh. In his defense, he thought he was telling the truth.

Tate laughed at the memory. Some other kid had argued he was wrong. He shut them down with his "facts."

— He probably got an A.

I think he did. Can I go to the wall with you two? We won't have to take one of the tourist buses. I'll have a driver.

—I'm sure I can talk her into it, especially if we don't have to ride the bus.

Good. Do you think we can go out for dinner, too? Maybe just the two of us?

—Probably, though I don't have a good idea of my schedule or if we will stay in Beijing or be doing something else.

A zing coursed through him. She'd agreed to a real date! On his personal coolness scale, it might beat the day his company had gone public. It would if the date happened. **We can play it by ear when I get there, then.**

—Falling asleep … Good night or good morning.

Tate checked the time. They'd chatted for almost an hour. He didn't even have to justify that it was better than the aerobics he'd missed because his heart felt better than everything else.

*P*aperwork. Not at all what Anne had pictured when she signed up to teach in China for the summer, though technically it wasn't *paper*work since it was all digital. Anne sat behind a computer sorting applications for the fall—a process the computer did semiautomatically. They'd sent Sophia to Shanghai to fill in for the teacher from Montana, who needed an emergency appendectomy. Anne taught for two hours each morning at a preschool. The children laughed at her attempts to speak to them in Mandarin and corrected her. After a week, she'd learned far more animals than Tate had in his app.

She hadn't heard from Tate since yesterday. As far as she could figure, he was flying to Beijing. As much as they joked about the time zone being a problem and being each other's past and future, the whole concept of when his flight left the States and when it was getting here skipping a day became rather confusing. A week of texting—every evening for her and every morning for him—and she was longing for a real conversation. There was a depth missing from their conversations. She hadn't realized what it was until she'd video chatted with her parents on Sunday. Never had she realized how much she relied on facial expressions and tone of voice for context in a conversation. Some texts had evolved into flirting, but she needed to see if the corners of his eyes crinkled, hear his laugh, and feel his hand hold hers. She didn't know him well enough to let her imagination fill in the details. From the texting, she knew the facts. He liked lasagna but not spaghetti. He had rooted for the Patriots in the Super Bowl, mostly because he didn't pay attention to football and knew they had a decent chance of winning. He had no intention of finishing his college degree, although he took online classes when he felt he needed more knowledge on the subject, and he thought pineapple was an acceptable pizza topping.

She knew more about him than about all the men she'd ever dated put together, but that wasn't what she wanted. Anne wanted to feel. Would there be another heated moment when he could follow through on a kiss?

"Williams Anne?" The front desk clerk stood at the desk where Anne worked, holding a vase of flowers.

"Yes?"

"This came for you." The clerk set them on the end of the desk.

Anne didn't have to look up the significance to know what red roses meant. She pulled the card out of the envelope.

> *Dinner?*
>
> *—B*

Anne opened her texting app. **Off at six—I mean 18:00. — I'll be outside the building. See you then.**

The next three hours were the longest of Anne's week. She went to the bathroom twice to see if she looked presentable. The slacks and polo shirt she'd worn today were hardly great date material, but it was thirty-five minutes by subway back to the apartment she shared with Sophia, until she left for Shanghai, and two other female employees. Why hadn't she expected this might happen? All she could do was brush her hair and apply lip gloss.

Finally, the digital clock on the wall read 18:00, and Anne shut down her computer for the night. Her roommates came by her desk.

"Flowers? Where did those come from?" asked Gwynn.

"I bet it is the guy she texts every night. I can't believe he paid to send you flowers. Are you going to take them back to the apartment? They would be difficult to manage on a crowded subway," said Becca.

Anne pulled out a single rose. "I thought about the subway and decided I would leave them here. I also won't be exploring with you tonight. Something has come up."

"No way. Mystery man is here?" asked Gwynn.

"He has business. He is taking me out tonight."

"Do we get to meet him?" asked Becca.

Anne slung her cross-body purse over her shoulder, then pushed her chair in and moved the vase to the center of her desk. "I don't know. He said he would pick me up outside. It may be one of those jump-in-the-car-at-the-curb things."

Gwynn and Becca followed Anne to the elevator.

Mitch stood in the lobby. Gwynn and Becca swooned, thinking it was Tate. Anne didn't correct them "Mitch, my roommates wanted to make sure a real man was picking me up. This is Gwynn, and this is Becca."

Thankfully Mitch caught on. "We need to hurry. The car is circling the block." He nodded at Gwynn and Becca and extended his arm.

As soon as they were out on the sidewalk, Anne apologized. "Sorry about that. After Xi'an, I felt I shouldn't mention his name so they'd have no idea who I was meeting."

"As his head of security, I say you made a good call." A black SUV pulled up, and Mitch opened the back door for her.

Anne's instinct was to jump into Tate's lap, but aware of the driver and Mitch, she slid in, buckled her seat belt, then reached for Tate's hand.

"You got the flowers." Tate pointed to the single rose she held.

"They are lovely. I think every woman in the office and a few of the men were dying of curiosity."

"Like the two women who watched you get into the car?" Tate looked back over his shoulder. Gwynn and Becca still stood on the sidewalk.

"They are my roommates. They know I text a mystery man every night, but they don't know his name. I let them believe Mitch was taking me out. Watching me get in the back seat and Mitch get in the front may have confused them." Everyone in the car laughed.

Mitch half turned in his seat. "I told Miss Williams she did the right thing." He turned back to the front.

Tate squeezed her hand. "I thought we'd go to Beihai Park. Besides spanning 171 acres, there is a lake where we can rent paddle boats. Mitch will give us as much privacy as we can get in a public place. Jared is already there."

"Does this mean you slept on the plane? I thought you would look more like the walking dead." Anne basked in his smile.

"Amazingly. All I needed was the proper motivation and something to dream about."

Anne felt herself blushing—a reaction she loved and hated for the same reason. Tate could tell what she felt.

Beihai Park was everything Tate hoped it would be—busy enough to keep everyone minding their own families and friends but not overcrowded. "I didn't ask, but are you fine with paddle boats? No seasickness?"

"I've never been on a paddleboat, but I have no problem canoeing." Anne looked up at him, anticipation in her eyes.

Jared waited at the dock area. "I rented that one for you." He pointed to a white swan with an awning. "I'll be in the yellow duck with Debi."

Tate helped Anne into the boat. She looked over her shoulder at Jared and the tall blonde next to him. "Who is Debi?"

"An addition to my security team." Tate put his feet on the pedals. "Ready?" They pushed off, then steered their way clear of the other docked boats.

"She is here because of me, isn't she?"

"Yes. Are you okay with that?" The few text conversations they'd had about bodyguards hadn't been adequate.

Anne bit her lip. "It's necessary to keep you safe."

"Us. You are a part of that now. Sadly, there are people who might try to use you."

"Am I safe on my own?"

"As far as Mitch can tell. Your name or photo hasn't shown up with mine on any blogs. One of the great things about China is that the locals have no clue I am not just another American tourist." Things would change once they were back in the States, but that could wait. That could wait until after the first kiss. The kiss he hoped would happen on this boat ride, wouldn't. They sat awkwardly on the hard plastic seats, the awning above them only giving them the illusion of privacy as Debi's binoculars were too often pointed in their direction.

"Dating you will not be easy, will it?"

"Five years ago, it would have been. Well, at least as easy as it would have been to date a poor college student who wouldn't look up from his computer."

Anne's laugh swirled around him. "So, equally difficult."

"From what I've seen, relationships are never easy. Do you know what you are getting into with me?"

"Not in the slightest, but no one ever does. I'm just hoping there is a place in your life that doesn't feel like Big Brother—or Big Sister—is watching." Anne nodded to the boat with Jared and Debi.

"There is. Just not here. They are trying to give us some privacy, which reminds me…" Tate pulled out the phone he'd programed for Anne. "Now we can talk. It isn't a satellite phone, but it has software that blocks prying ears, though only if you call another phone that has the same software."

"So, basically, I can only call you?" She took the flip phone from him and opened it. She'd never seen anything like it—a smartphone screen that folded in half.

"And Mitch, Jared, and Debi. Their numbers are programed in, but you shouldn't need to call them."

"I need to get used to the bodyguard thing, too." Anne turned the phone over in her hands. "Will it be better back in the US?"

"Yes and no. There are places where I can be alone, places I can go to unwind. Then there are places where I must have a bevy of bodyguards. They guard my home at all times, but only the outside. If I stay out of the home gym, I can avoid seeing them for days."

"So, if you had a video date night, there would be people watching you?"

"No more than in any other house with a home-security system. Doors and windows monitored. No video, no audio." Tate turned the boat away from the shore.

Anne studied the white pagoda and shoreline for several minutes before turning back to him. "If our relationship ends badly, what happens to me?"

"I don't know. I never thought of that. What would you want to happen?"

"If I am seen with you often, I will lose my privacy, become a public figure. I won't be able to teach second grade anymore. The stakes are higher than if I am going out with the boy next door or the junior high basketball coach."

They fell into silence. *What just happened?* The plan had been for a first kiss, not a breakup. Not that the conversation had ruined the kiss. It was more about his paid watchers. "So, what now?"

Anne stopped pedaling. "I'm not sure. Can we finish today the way you planned? You have meetings for the next two days, and I can think about this—about us."

"So are we still on for the wall?"

Anne turned to face him, her eyes betraying nothing. "Can I get back to you on that?"

Tate could only nod.

14

$\mathcal{A}$lone in the room she had shared with Sophia the first few days in Beijing, Anne longed to talk to someone other than her roommates, who did nothing but talk about how tall and rugged Mitch looked and about the apparent age difference. Honestly, it had never occurred to Anne that Mitch was most likely ten years older, because she defined him by his job.

Texting Sophia would take too long. And Mom would be at work. Besides, the last idea wasn't helpful because Anne had only mentioned Tate once in a conversation about the apology. She felt her parents should know that much at least. Unlike her sister, Anne was never one to share the nuances of her relationships with her family and only occasionally the heartbreaks.

Need to talk about B. Video chat when you can. Hopefully that would be enough for Sophia to know they needed to talk in code. Five minutes later, the video-chat icon sounded.

"Hey! I love Shanghai. Look at my mini apartment." Sophia turned her phone around the entirety of an apartment that couldn't have been more than ten feet by ten feet square. "There's my bathroom. Everything's technically inside my shower. So the entire room gets cleaned every day. The kitchen sink is the size of one of my mother's salad bowls, but the hot plate works great. The other teachers share a space larger than this with bunk beds. Since they are both guys, I got put here. The school keeps the apartment for visiting parents and guests. Good news! Mr. Montana cowboy will be back to teaching Monday, he thinks, so I'll be back Monday night. They want me to stay to make sure he can make it through the day. I guess he had a bad reaction to some medication. Anyway, I can see you haven't been crying, but you look like you could. What did he do?"

"He did nothing. He sent me flowers and planned a date. He even figured out a way to get us some privacy. We just got talking about his lifestyle, and it raises questions. I don't know if I can live in a fishbowl. He has a new associate whose job is the same as J's, only he hired her because of me."

"Wait. Does she follow you?"

"No, but if we got serious, it could be a thing, like that woman in Indiana who dated that Daniel guy out of Chicago. And don't tell me you don't remember. You followed a couple of those blogs when you crushed on him."

Sophia's lips twisted as if she were pretending to think hard. "Never see Daniel and his wife in the papers anymore. At least not much. I think they even have a child. But Daniel was out living the life, going to events, even lived a bad-boy life in college. B isn't like that. He goes to a few charity things. Hasn't dated any movie stars. Compared to what it could be, his life is rather quiet."

"But what will my life be like? And what happens if I go to those charity gala things and then we break up? It isn't like I can just consume a few quarts of ice cream. People will be watching."

"Maybe for a while. But what do you want to do? If he is your one and only, is it worth the risk?"

"I don't know. That is why I asked you to call."

"I can't give you the answers. You've dated enough of the wrong types of guys to know what doesn't fit. Take away the lifestyle difference and would you fit? The rest can be worked out. That is one advantage of his life—a private island is always a possibility."

"But how do I know?" Anne knew the question had no answer.

"You know I am terrible at this, right? I've been in love with a guy since high school and live vicariously through celebrity crushes, making me one messed-up person. I have no idea how you should know."

"I told him I'm taking two days off from the relationship. It has only been two hours since our date ended, and I want to text him. Does that mean something?"

"Maybe . . . I have an idea. Write all the times and things you want to talk to him about."

"Considering I haven't been able to talk to him about half the things I want to, that is a lot. I want to just see a video and hold his hand without Mitch telling us to hold hands. I want to be 100 percent certain there is chemistry."

"No kiss yet?"

"Of course not. It isn't like he can even walk me to the door. Bodyguards are a serious drawback."

"I think that has more to do with where you live than anything. If you were at home, he could walk you to the door and—" Sophia made a kissing face.

Anne rolled her eyes.

"That is what you want to do, isn't it? You've met on some intellectual level, you think he is funny, but you need to know . . ."

"A guy can be a great kisser but not have the rest of the connections." Anne raised her brows at Sophia. "How many gallons of ice cream have we shared over relationship fails? He may not even be really interested in me."

"He wouldn't have brought a female bodyguard if he wasn't interested."

Anne let that sink in. "Do you think our relationship could all be based on his guilt for the past and he is more in love with the idea of me?"

"If he is, it will be like kissing your brother."

"Yuck." Anne shuddered. "That was not helpful. But you have given me something to think about. The biggest problem is we are officially only three dates in and I am trying to make a life-time choice."

Sophia yawned. Anne mirrored the action. "Good night," they said in unison.

Anne flipped open her new phone. No texts. Not that she expected any with the look on his face when she'd asked for time. Her thumbs hovered over the keys. No, it was only two days. If she missed him already, that was kind of an answer, wasn't it?

The meetings were a disaster. After months of negotiations, they'd brought up yet another concern. Before starting this business *adventure*—it was too convoluted to be a venture—Tate read in an online business magazine that it could take months to negotiate and that there would be tests and circular negotiations, and he thought he was prepared to face the process. He looked at Jared, who shook his head imperceptibly. Walking out wasn't an option. Tate didn't care. He stood up.

"By now you have seen and read enough to reverse engineer my product. If you don't, you know how to reach me. I'll be in Beijing a couple more days."

Jared followed Tate out of the room. Neither spoke until they were in the SUV.

"That wasn't your plan."

Tate opened a bottle of water. "No. But I couldn't just sit through another round of the same twenty items we discussed at our first meeting. The only difference now is we don't have an interpreter in the room."

"I think this has less to do with them and more to do with whatever did or didn't happen last night in the park."

"Probably." Tate didn't want to discuss Anne. "But we aren't going there."

"Where are we going?"

"How about Hong Kong?" A day and a half where he wasn't so closely monitored sounded heavenly.

"Should I leave Debi here?"

They were back to Anne. "I don't know. Whatever Mitch thinks."

Jared frowned. "As a friend, I think you need to get your head on straight. As one of your overpaid employees, I *know* you do. She made a smart choice last night. Being your friend isn't easy. The only thing that makes it manageable for me is that anyone who looks at me sees an employee. No one bothers me. Girlfriend? Wife? That would be insanely different. Some of those women who chase you already live in that world—or think they want to."

"I need to make this right."

"You can't. Anne needs to choose you on her own. Look at the bright side: she isn't blinded by your money like—" Jared stopped short of mentioning Tate's college girlfriend. They'd started dating just as Lingo-mi had become a success and Tate had taken the semester off to put his energy into the company and developing more language models. She'd turned down the 1.5 carat diamond ring he'd purchased and accused him of being a skinflint. She wanted the ring more than she wanted him.

"You have a point. Let's go to Hong Kong, then. That should make our hosts wonder. You know they have someone tailing us, don't you?"

"Of course. Do you need your bags, or should we head for the airport?"

"Mitch won't be happy if I take off, especially without a plan."

"If we stay at the same hotel you did last time and don't go clubbing or something stupid, it should be fine."

"I never go clubbing."

"See? Mitch has nothing to worry about. I'll book us a flight. You call him and tell him our plan."

Tate swiped his phone open. "You would take the easy task."

Mitch answered on the first ring. "I'd ask if the meeting was over, but you two left fifteen minutes ago." Tate wasn't surprised his head of security knew that.

"I'm going to Hong Kong until Friday night. Jared is booking a flight. Planning on lying low and being a tourist."

"I see." Mitch's disapproving tone carried a mini lecture. "Should I meet you?"

Jared turned and held up three fingers. "12:50 flight."

"Looks like Jared got you a ticket. I guess Debi will stay here."

"Good, I want her to talk with Anne. That woman gets lost more than anyone I have ever seen. Even if you don't date her, a lecture on personal safety is long overdue."

"She can't be that bad."

"Debi said she tried to get on the subway in the wrong direction this morning—again. Her roommate stopped her. If she had to navigate Beijing alone, who knows where she would end up."

Tate smiled. Anne would have been a terrible Girl Scout. Chen Lǎoshī had scolded her more than once for taking too long on a bathroom break. Like the other students, he'd wondered how she could have gotten lost coming back, even if the display-case theme had changed. "See you at the airport. I am sure Jared will text you the info." He ended the call and stared at his phone. Should he text Anne?

The driver pulled up at the terminal before Tate could decide. With no luggage, they easily cleared security. At the gate, Tate pulled out his phone once more. Someone announced the boarding call in several languages. Tate settled into his seat. It was either now or in three hours and forty minutes.

Went to Hong Kong. I'll be back for Great Wall. Have a good day.

He hit send as the flight attendant announced the doors were closing. He reread the message. He'd sent more personal messages to his office assistant. Tate stuffed his phone back in his pocket and prepared to spend the flight kicking himself.

It was hard to miss Debi, arms crossed, standing to one side of the elevator Friday night. The tall blonde stood out like a sunflower in a field of poppies. "Got a minute?"

Anne nodded, and her roommates stopped with her.

"Do you have plans for tonight? If not, I think we should talk." Debi uncrossed her arms and moved toward the lobby. Her face betrayed no emotion. Had something happened to Tate? He hadn't texted back after she replied a quick '**See you Saturday**' to his short text Thursday around lunchtime.

The roommates followed them. Anne turned to them. "This is my friend Debi. And these are my roommates, Gwynn and Becca."

"I've seen you the last couple days. Have you been following us?" Gwynn narrowed her eyes, and Becca nodded.

"You've been following me?" At six foot two, Debi was impossible to miss. Especially in a sea of Chinese faces, but Anne didn't recall seeing her at all.

A slow smile spread over Debi's face. "You are fairly easy to tail, even if you take the most scenic of routes."

Both roommates laughed. Gwynn recovered first. "When Sophia left for Shanghai, she warned us not to let you out of our sight."

"I'm not that bad."

Gwynn crossed her arms. "So why follow you if she is a friend and not just coming up and saying hi like a normal person?"

Anne scrambled for an answer. "It is a game we play…long story. Sorry if we weirded you out. I'll catch up with you guys later."

Gwynn and Becca left after a round of goodbyes.

"Gwynn is still suspicious." Instead of leaving the building, Debi headed for a seating area. "I'll give her a few minutes to give up following us."

"Why are you here?" Anne perched on the edge of a seat.

"Because I have a guess about what happened Wednesday night between you and Tate, and if I am right, I'm the best person to answer your questions. Also to give you some pointers. No offense, but you should've noticed me more than a half dozen times in the past two days. I was trying to make a game of getting caught."

"My father says I am the least observant person he knows. I'd say it is not true, but obviously it is, to some extent. And you're right. I have questions for you."

"Let's go find some dinner and take a walk around the Forbidden City, which is aptly named as a good portion of it is off-limits." Debi led the way out of the building.

"So, why were you following me?"

"To do a risk assessment."

Anne groaned. "I failed, didn't I?"

"Despite your lack of direction and observation, no. You carry yourself with confidence and are aware of your personal space, which doesn't make you a target. Someone would need to follow you for a while to realize you don't always know where you are going."

"I always know where I am going. I just get there in the least predictable way."

Debi laughed. "That is an excellent way of putting it. One thing in your favor in China is your ability to blend in—something I personally don't experience anyplace other than the NCAA women's basketball finals. Back home, depending on where you are, I'm betting you have some of the same issues I have here in China."

"The minority issues?"

"Pretty much, but not as bad—although in a small town in Alabama or Idaho, you would stand out more than in Boston or San Francisco. But we don't have to worry about that now. Tate won't burden you with full-time bodyguards until there is a reason to. Another benefit of being in China—some American social media and news is blocked. Even if someone posted a photo of you two together, the locals wouldn't see it. And unless they already know you, the chances of someone finding you are low. Tate isn't popular enough to warrant the Chinese version of paparazzi." Debi stopped in front of a noodle stand. "Dinner?"

Both women ordered. "So, if Tate doesn't have a paparazzi problem, why does he need bodyguards?"

Debi tapped her chin. "Same reason he gave you that phone. His business here garners attention from certain sectors."

"Oh." Anne hoped she was reading between the lines correctly—either the businesses or some bureaucrat thought Tate was worth keeping tabs on.

"Then there is the occasional tourist."

"We ran into two of those two weekends ago in Xi'an. So, my first question is how much will having you guys around disrupt my life?"

"Tate's estate has a detached control room. There are always at least two people there. The biggest threats he has are women who try climbing the fence to get to him and a few people who desperately want him to look at their ideas. We monitor the house much like any security system. When he is in residence, only the outside entrances are monitored. Tate could be running around the house dressed as a giant hamster and we wouldn't know about it. There are panic buttons in various locations in case something happens. To be honest, if not for the women trying to get to him, it would be the second most boring job I've ever had. Tate isn't super social, so his outings are few and far between."

"So we could have a seminormal dating experience?"

"If you are discreet about where you go, then yes. But I'd say you'd have a lot of dates and private parties. Going to a baseball game or a movie's opening night, not so much. Best wait until the film is ready to leave the theaters. Restaurants that require reservations or fast-food places where people think he just reminds them of him are generally low risk, because why would a billionaire go to the Golden Arches?"

"What about that woman a couple years ago who dated that Chicago billionaire? Her life was turned upside down when she first got outed to the press."

"Her case was handled poorly. It didn't help that Daniel Crawford had been on the front page of several magazines touting him as one of the most eligible bachelors. Plus, there was a lawsuit with Summerset What's-Her-Nose. His face was at every checkout stand in America. Tate's lack of social life and an abundance of Hollywood A-listers doing stupid things keeps him out of the limelight. A carefully orchestrated unveiling of your relationship to the public should keep things buried on page three of the entertainment section." Debi found a trash can for her empty container.

"You sound more like a PR rep than a bodyguard." Anne pulled some wipes from her purse and cleaned her hands.

"I need to keep my options open. I can't spend my entire life tackling crazies if I want to have a long-term relationship. I want to be a mother someday."

Anne jumped on the change of subject. "Anyone in particular?"

"Maybe. Now, there is a subway station. I want you to get us back to your place."

"But I've never been here before."

"That is the point. Can you read a map, or is that related to your sense of direction?"

"I think I can."

With only one minor detour, which Debi pointed out didn't make them backtrack, they made it. It just wasn't the most direct route, and they arrived at the apartment forty minutes later than they would have otherwise.

"Will you be with us tomorrow at the Great Wall?"

Debi nodded. "It gives us that two-American-couples cover. I think Mitch has chosen a less busy section of the wall, but it is still bound to be crowded with tourists."

"Then I have a favor to ask, if it is possible ..." Anne made her request so quietly even the best surveillance equipment would have had a hard time picking it up.

Debi smiled. "I'll give it my best. See you tomorrow."

The day and a half in Hong Kong wasn't as rejuvenating as Tate hoped, though it had the desired effect on the company with which he was negotiating. They emailed new contracts to his lawyers with details of an acceptable venture. He should have walked out earlier.

Tate spent most of his time in Hong Kong finding things he wanted to show Anne. Perhaps when her summer teaching contract ended, he could convince her to take a few days' vacation with him there, where the surveillance didn't feel as heavy. The late-night flight back to Beijing produced a nightmare that had him being tossed over the side of the Great Wall. The fact that Anne had recruited his bodyguards to help with the deed left him in the middle of falling when he woke up.

A couple blocks from Anne's, they stopped to buy breakfast from a street vendor. Debi left the men in the car and walked over to the high-rise apartment to get Anne. When they pulled up to the curb in front of the building, Debi and Anne were laughing. Wasn't this how his nightmare had started?

Anne hopped into the back seat but didn't reach for his hand as she exchanged greetings with everyone. Tate tried not to analyze the reasons. Jared passed around warm jiaozi—dumplings filled with pork and vegetables—and napkins. Maybe Debi had told her about the food...that would be a good reason not to hold hands. Soon the food was gone. Anne offered Tate a hand wipe from the recesses of her purse, then she pulled out a small notebook and pen. She found a blank page.

I don't really want to talk in front of them.

She handed the notebook and pen over as she laughed at a story Debi was telling. Tate wrote back.

I understand. So, we are reduced to the old-fashioned version of texting?

Kind of. We don't need to use emojis.
Her handwriting was neat and not overly loopy.
Tate answered some question Debi had asked about the wall.

This is still awkward, isn't it? I've missed our texting. I thought of calling you since we can call now.

Calling would be nice—much more personal.

Did you ask Debi to come speak to me?

Tate's eyebrows touched the hair on his forehead. He tried to erase his reaction before anyone noticed.

When? About what?

She said she had been doing an assessment on me. Wondered if I was always so misoriented in my travels. We also talked about how a client-dating relationship worked from her perspective as a bodyguard.

Oh. That would be interesting.

It is information I needed.

And?

Our talk was very helpful.

Not the answer he was hoping for. If he had been in a boardroom, he would have asked the tough questions and pushed for answers.

I missed you when I was in Hong Kong.

Thanks for giving me time to think. I can tell you are having a hard time waiting, but I'd rather talk than write my conclusions.

We are going to a section of the wall where you can hike to another section. It takes about three hours. Jared said not many people make the hike because of the stairs. I figured it should give us space to talk as they won't need to be too near.

Good thing I brought my good shoes.

Up to this point, Anne had passed the notebook in a way that prevented contact. This time when she passed the notebook, their hands touched. Anne didn't let go, and electric sparks flew between their fingertips. It surprised Tate that the notebook didn't burst into flames. Tate took the notebook with his left hand and captured Anne's with his right. The smile she gave him was better than any emoji.

They didn't write any more as the driver sped, not nearly fast enough, toward their destination.

Tour buses and vehicles of all descriptions crowded the roads the closer they got to the wall. If this was the least congested of spots near the Beijing part of the wall, the others must be insanely busy. Vendor stalls lined the area where the SUV dropped them off. The driver would meet them at their exit point.

"How many tourists think they are getting a good deal?" Tate asked in Mandarin, nodding to a group of Americans that must have come from one of the tour buses.

"Sophia and I learned I get a different price than she does before I open my mouth, as long as I don't have my tourist purse with me." Anne continued to hold his hand. A good sign.

Tate had seen videos of the Great Wall but somehow missed the massive number of steps. After the second staircase, the crowds thinned. Older people and visitors with children seemed unwilling to chance a third set.

As the flow of tourists thinned to a trickle, Mitch widened the gap, hiking at an inhuman pace. Jared and Debi fell behind by a dozen yards, also attempting to give them some privacy. Ahead, Mitch disappeared around a turn in the wall. He reappeared when the wall turned again a few minutes later.

"I think it is time I give you my answer." Anne led him around the turn and down a short flight of steps. The jog in the wall gave them the illusion of being alone. At the bottom, Anne turned and put her hand on the center of his chest, then rose up on her toes. Her lips were warm as they pressed against his. Tate dropped his hand to her waist and pulled her closer, deepening their connection. Anne's fingers slipped around his head and into his hair. She murmured something against his lips before letting go.

"Would you mind explaining that again?"

Anne blushed. Had the sunlight not been on her, he might not have noticed the change. "That isn't how I intended to tell you, but I think I would like to try and see where this goes."

Tate calculated he had maybe thirty seconds to answer before his bodyguard-chaperones interrupted them. He brushed a kiss over Anne's lips once, then twice. The third time, he lingered and deepened it, half listening for the inevitable interruption. At the sound of Debi's laughter, he pulled back.

Anne looked over her shoulder. "I think our moment of privacy is over."

"Good thing we have miles of wall to cover. I bet we can find another spot. Hiking the unrestored part isn't on most tourists' lists." Tate followed the line of the wall to the horizon. One of those guard huts might be nice to explore...

Debi and Jared came around the corner. "We have some loud tourists behind us. They are moving slowly, but you two need to get a move on if you are going to catch up to Mitch."

Debi raised her brows. Anne could almost hear her asking if she'd given them enough time. She answered with the tiniest of nods. Tate looked from Anne to Debi and back before taking Anne's hand and proceeding along the wall.

Tate leaned in close. "Should I ask what is up with you and Debi?"

"I asked her if she could arrange a few minutes alone for us. I wanted to tell you my thoughts on our relationship."

"I haven't heard you say much about that."

Anne swatted his arm. "I think you got the general message. I know it won't be easy to get more stolen kisses and text messages for the next little while. Even when we get back to the US, it could be complicated. I have a classroom of second graders on the East Coast, and you have a building full of tech people on the West."

"I'm sure we can work it out. I've been putting off buying a jet of my own, but now...and there is a need for teachers in Seattle too."

"You would purchase a jet so we can visit easier?"

"Seems like a good investment to me."

They reached another flight of uneven stone steps. Anne appreciated how Tate helped her without babying her because of her size and how he didn't leave her behind because she was slow on the uneven ones.

The view from the top of the stairs took her breath away. The stone wall snaked as far as the eye could see in either direction. "Do you know what one of the best things about the wall is?"

Tate grinned down at her. "Vacant guard buildings?"

Maybe that too. They could test one later. "I was thinking more along the lines of I know where I am going and can't get lost."

"That's good because I don't want to lose you."

A warmth having nothing to do with the heat of the day filled Anne. She squeezed Tate's hand and continued hiking.

Anne slid the alarm on her phone to snooze so she could have a few more minutes to replay the weekend in her mind. The three bodyguards had managed to give Anne and Tate a few more quick moments, none of them in one of the guardhouses. Which might have been good. Tate's kisses were more potent than she'd expected, and the way he smiled whenever they snuck a kiss was equally as devastating. It was all the fireworks of Chinese New Year packed into seventy seconds. He would be in meetings all day. Tonight, he'd arranged for them to have dinner, and tomorrow he would be gone again. At least this time they could talk on the phone.

Her phone rang. The regular one. It wasn't Tate.

"Good morning?"

"Miss Williams? This is Mr. Peters. We have a problem. The teacher with the appendectomy needs to return home because of complications, and his co-teacher has volunteered to fly with him. So he will be out for the next week. How fast can you pack and get to Beijing South station?"

"I need an hour to pack." Anne sprung out of bed.

"I'll meet you there at 7:40 with tickets and the information you need. Look for me at the main ticket counter."

Either Gwynn or Becca was already in the shower, so Anne settled for washing her face and arms before racing around her room packing. This packing job was marginally better than the one she did upon leaving Xi'an.

"Hey, what's going on?" asked Gwynn, hair wrapped in a towel.

"Mr. Peters called. He needs me in Shanghai with Sophia. The teachers he had there are flying back to the US. I'm supposed to be at the south train station by 7:40."

"I'll tell Becca to hurry and get dressed so we can go with you. No offense, but if I tell you to turn right and go to the station, you'll go left."

"I know. Thanks. I will leave my office-uniform polos here." Anne rehung the four shirts as Gwynn disappeared.

Anne's phone beeped. Sophia. **Yay! We get to teach together again! The cowboys gave me the keys to their apartment. We've been playing musical stuff since 4:00 a.m.**

I'm taking the train. I'll let you know when I should arrive.

Anne shouldered her other phone and dialed Tate.

"Good morning, beautiful." His voice was gravelly and sent a chill down her spine. Her phone slipped. She caught it but dropped her folded T-shirts on the floor.

"Sorry to call so early. I am leaving for Shanghai within the hour—an emergency with a sick teacher."

"So you are being Shanghaied from our date?" His voice was more alert.

"I guess you could make that very bad pun this early in the morning and I'll excuse it."

Tate's laugh warmed her.

"I need to finish packing. Call tonight?"

"Definitely. Be safe."

"You too." It was on the tip of her tongue to say more, but the call disconnected. It was crazy to want to say things like that already.

They made it to the station at 7:25. Mr. Peters waited at the counter. "Good, you made it. If there are tickets left for the 7:50, you should be able to get through security and to your train."

He turned and spoke with the ticketing employee, then turned back to Anne with a ticket. "Best I could do is the 8:10, so you won't have to run to get through security. Here is your information packet on the school. We'll decide at the end of the week who will finish out the term in Shanghai. They loved having our Texas and Montana cowboys at the school. It was a true novelty having tall men who can rope cattle and chairs."

Anne waved her goodbyes to her roommates and Mr. Peters and followed the signs, printed in both Chinese and English, through security and to her train. To her surprise, they seated her in the pricier and more comfortable business-class car. A meal was even included—a bonus to the jiǎozi she'd grabbed from a vendor on the walk to the station. She leaned back and relaxed, only to have her phone beep.

Mom had started her message with a worried-face emoji. **Didn't hear from you this weekend. You missed the video call. Are you all right?**

Sorry, Mom. The weekend got crazy. I meant to text you. Right now I am on the world's fastest train to Shanghai. Anne debated telling Mom about the real reason she'd missed making the call last night.

—I thought you just got transferred to Beijing.

A teacher had an emergency appendectomy. Things didn't go well, and he is headed back to the States. Another teacher is accompanying him, so I am off to teach again. Three schools (and office work) in four weeks. I must be setting a record. I am getting to see more of China than I thought I would. Go bucket list!

—So, what did you do this weekend?

We went to the Great Wall.

—We? I thought Sophia was in Shanghai already.

She is. Remember Bertram Gilman?

— The mean boy in seventh grade and who's now $$$$?

Yup. I went with him.

— What? Why?

Because I really like him.

— I am having one of those mom moments when I want to video chat with you.

MOM, NO! Public train.

— Fine. Call me tonight. I don't care what time it is here.

Okay. But keep it to yourself. Dad only. No siblings, no friends, no social media.

— My lips and fingers are sealed. Love you!

If Anne had a things-I-wish-I-hadn't-done bucket list, she would add telling her mom about Tate while on the train as number one. The call tonight would be worse.

The contract was finalized. Tate wanted to sign and go home, but the CEO of Wang International wanted a photo op and was making it a big deal. Since tomorrow was July 4 and they considered four unlucky and a major US holiday, the signing would wait until the sixth. Six was a lucky number, especially for starting a new business. Tate texted his office administrator and asked to have his flights and hotels changed. He would be in Beijing until Friday morning. **Also, please arrange to go to Shanghai on Friday for the weekend. We can fly back on Monday. Shanghai add-on is personal. Bill me accordingly.**

— No problem. I'll send details as soon as I have them. Plane or train to Shanghai?

Either.

Tate put his phone away and reassured the CEO the necessary arrangements were being made on his end. The government office announced a celebratory dinner for that evening. Tate accepted the invitation, then went through all the formalities before escaping to his hotel for the afternoon. At least Anne had already canceled their date tonight. He wasn't sure if she was prepared to be included in the publicity surrounding the celebrations of the next few days. The photos would find their way to more than just social media, earning him notice in every corner of the country. He checked his watch. Likely Anne was still on the train.

Hey, our contract is a go. I am staying in Beijing through Thursday. Do you mind if I come to Shanghai before flying back to the States?

— That sounds like fun. You probably won't be back this summer, will you?

Not for a few weeks. But I'll try to work something out.

— So see you Friday night?

Definitely.

— Train is almost here. Talk tonight? <3

Maybe late. Dinner with CEO.

— K

With the contract a go, Tate turned his attention, or most of it, to other business matters, while his heart counted the beats until Friday.

Tate refused the offered liquor, again. After months of talks and dinners, did no one understand that he never drank, ever? A woman draped herself across his arm. She was the second to try that tonight.

Debi moved in, giving the woman a practiced glare. "Too bad you couldn't bring a date. These women don't see me as a threat." She linked her arm through his.

Jared leaned over from his seat on the other side of Debi and tapped his watch.

Tate answered with a shrug. It was hard to tell what the business protocols were for such social occasions. After three hours, the party showed no signs of ending. It was the longest meal event they had been treated to thus far. The women to his right changed with every course. If it wasn't considered rude, Tate would have sent a "Wish you were here" text to Anne a dozen times by now. A week of this and he might lose his mind.

Another woman sat down in the chair to his right, but she didn't grab him or flirt outrageously. Perhaps if he spoke to this one, she would stay and keep the others away.

"I am Wang Xiyu Ying, daughter of Wang Wei."

The hair on Tate's arm stood up. The CEO was her father. That explained why her manners were better; however, it didn't mean she wasn't chasing him for his money. But he could not treat her with disrespect.

"Nice to meet you. Where did you go to school?"

"I start my master's degree at Princeton in the fall."

Tate nodded and spent as much time as possible looking at his food as he kept up a light conversation. When the final course was cleared, Tate realized he had only a vague sense of what he had eaten. Drinks were passed around again.

The CEO frowned at Tate's team's refusal to drink. "Surely you can celebrate with us once?"

"In the words of a wise grandfather, 'Not even once.'" Tate added a slight bow, not completely sure if it was necessary.

"You speak of your grandfather with much reverence."

"He was a great man who taught me much."

The CEO gestured to the room. "What would he think of this?"

"He would think I should not drink with you."

There was an uncomfortable laugh, but then the CEO joined in. "Then you have passed the last test. You did not compromise. This means I deal with an honest man."

Test? Seriously? Tate had never read about this sort of test in any of the business journals or blogs. What was the appropriate reaction? "Thank you, Wang Wei, for your hospitality this evening. We hope you will excuse us, but our associates in the US are just heading into the office, and we would like to ask our employees to prepare for the signing of our contract as well."

His answer seemed satisfactory, and the meeting broke up. As soon as Tate belted himself into the back seat of the SUV, he opened his phone and texted Anne.

Sorry it is so late. I thought dinner would never end!

— That's okay. I had an interesting phone call with my mother. She asked many questions I didn't want to answer over the video chat, this being China and all.

You can use this phone to call them.

— Thanks. I wasn't sure. Not that it would have helped the call. I don't often tell my parents about my boyfriends.

Tate wanted to explore that topic, though not by text. **Can I call in a half hour?**

— Sorry, our one-room apartment doesn't give me anyplace to go. Sophia is already sleeping. My bathroom has a Western-style toilet and sink inside the shower stall, and I am not talking to you from in there.

That sounds uncomfortable.

—I am sure it is functional and cuts down on the cleaning. I need to be at the school by eight tomorrow. I should try to get some sleep.

Good night, then. Hope to catch you tomorrow.

The Shanghai school was more relaxed than the one in Xi'an. And Anne wasn't the first Asian American to teach there. The teachers talked to Sophie and Anne during lunch and after school, swapping ideas and stories and practicing English. Most of the teachers had attended residential schools as children and had no concerns with the system. One even thought American discipline problems could be linked to too-frequent visiting with family—a view Anne couldn't wrap her mind around. She might not tell her family everything about her life, but they were always there for her. Her brother, Gareth, might tease her about getting lost finding her feet, but he'd literally stood between her and a bully when she was in third grade and in less-physical ways since. She might not look like her sisters, but that didn't keep them from dressing the same for Halloween or wearing matching dresses to church on Easter Sunday.

Anne contemplated this as she walked down one of the food streets Thursday night after school with several other of the teachers who were intent on introducing Anne and Sophia to some of the usual flavors and sights. Anne caught only a portion of what was being said. In a country where she blended in, she didn't belong. Nothing was familiar, and no one was greeting her with welcoming arms. When she'd put China on her bucket list years ago, she'd thought it would feel like going home. But it didn't. A sudden, overwhelming homesickness filled her. It had only been three days since she'd talked with her mom, but she wanted to talk to her again. No matter what she and Tate did this weekend, she wasn't going to miss the call.

They passed a shop with a television in the window. A news program played.

"Look at that hot American!" Anne wasn't sure which of the teachers said it. On the screen, Tate was shaking hands with an older man in a business suit.

"Isn't that interesting? Some American businessman making a deal with a Chinese businessman—must be a slow news day." Sophia tried to get the group to move along.

"But not just any American. Gilman Tate is very rich and made app to help teach English better. All Chinese will have access. Very important news."

"Isn't CEOs daughter lucky? Look how close she stands to Gilman Tate."

Too close for Anne, but it was a photo op. She tamped down the green seeds of jealousy.

The teachers continued to talk about Tate as the next story came on.

Sophia shoulder-bumped Anne. "Look, Xiao Long Bao!" The broth-filled pork dumplings had made both women's top-ten list of vendor foods. Anne bought one before moving on to a more adventurous food.

One teacher pointed to a stack of bamboo leaves tied in triangles. "Must try Zongzi—traditional for dragon boat festival. Over now, but he still sells."

"What is in them?" asked Sophia.

"Rice and either red bean or pork and maybe spices."

Much less intimidating than a fried starfish. Anne and Sophia both purchased one.

"Imagine trying to fill these." Anne waited for one of the teachers to eat theirs first, unsure if she was supposed to eat the leaves as well. She was relieved to see the teachers remove the leaves and drizzle the contents with honey. She added them to her safe-foods list.

They passed stalls of more exotic foods. The teachers laughed at the faces Sophia made at a few of the booths. No way, no how, were fried beetle grubs making it onto any dinner menu. Neither were live, drunken shrimp.

"I won't try either," whispered the shortest of the teachers.

Several of the teachers lived in the same building Sophia and Anne did, and they headed home together. "No, take this train." The oldest of the teachers pointed to a different subway line. "Tonight is a clear night. You must see from other side."

They came up on the opposite side of the bay to a crowded walkway. Sophia and Anne followed the other teachers.

"So many of the buildings are brightly lit. Look at the Oriental Pearl. I didn't realize the lights changed." Sophia raised her phone to take a video.

"That is Shanghai Tower, second tallest building in the world." The shortest teacher pointed across the bay. "It is much taller than your famous Empire State Building."

Anne didn't mention that there were several buildings taller than the Empire State Building.

"Do lovers meet at the top of it too?" Sophia's question carried a dash of sassiness.

"What do you mean?"

"Many iconic American romance movies, such as *Affair to Remember*, *Sleepless in Seattle*, and *Enchanted* have pivotal love scenes at the building." Sophia took a selfie.

"Or it held the fate of the world." Anne added in whisper, sure that some superhero movies and Percy Jackson weren't on the Chinese streaming sites.

The women returned to their apartment building just before ten. Unlike in Xi'an, there was no curfew or watchful guard. Anne's phone rang as they opened the door.

"Hi, Tate."

Sophia made a schmoozy face, grabbed her towel, and pointed to the bathroom, indicating she was going to take a shower. They learned it was better to take their showers at night so they could get ready in the morning without having the wet walls dampen their clothes as they put on their makeup or brushed their teeth.

"Hey, I missed you today."

"Really? It looked like you had plenty of company," Anne teased.

"Ha, ha. I think Wang Xiu Ying's father wants me as a son-in-law. Considering multicultural marriages are not always viewed kindly, I assume my net worth is the reason. Debi had to run quite a bit of interference during the after-party."

"Congratulations on getting the contract finished."

"Had I not run away to Hong Kong last week, I don't know that it would have happened."

"So my asking you for a couple days was a good thing?" Anne pulled out her pajamas and decided what to wear to work tomorrow.

"That would be stretching it. We had to change our plans for coming to Shanghai tomorrow—some formalities with the local government. But we got bullet-train tickets and should be there by 17:30. Do you want to meet me someplace around six or make my driver find your apartment building?"

"How many chaperones do we get?"

Tate laughed. "Just the usual suspects. I was on Chinese National TV tonight, but we don't expect that to change things."

"We saw you. The women around me were saying how handsome you were."

"Do you think I'm handsome?"

Anne rolled her eyes and wished it was a video call so he could see her face. "Maybe. So, should I bring Sophia since we will already be a crowd?"

"Sure. If she wants to come."

"Oh, she will. Neither of us knows how long we are here for."

Sophia exited the bathroom, her hair wrapped in a towel."

"So where shall we meet?" asked Tate.

"Just a second." Anne pulled the phone from her ear and got Sophia's attention. "Tate wants to meet us around six. Ideas on where?"

"I get to go on your date?" Sophia put her toiletries on a shelf.

"You and the rest of the entourage."

"What about the top of Shanghai Tower?" Sophia made a heart symbol with her hands.

Anne put the phone back to her ear. "Did you hear that?"

"Top, or rather, observation deck, of the Shanghai Tower at six. And since she's out of the shower, I guess I missed my chance to flirt outrageously with you."

Anne leaned her head against her shoulder, trapping the phone. "Pretty much."

"Then I must wait until tomorrow. And I will get Jared to find us a way to have a few moments alone."

Anne knew she was blushing and kept her eyes on the floor. Sophia kindly stayed on the other side of the ten-by-ten room. "I'd like that. Night, Tate."

"Night, sweetheart."

Anne tucked her phone away.

Sophia stopped towel drying her hair. "Look at you. You're glowing. If that isn't a woman in love, I don't know what is."

"Thanks for taking a shower to give me some talk time."

"I'll sacrifice and take the first shower anytime."

Anne laughed. The person who took the last shower got to the dry toilet and everything else. "You do realize that meeting him on top of the Shanghai Tower will not be movie romantic, right?" Anne counted on her fingers. "One, huge crowds. Two, one of the fastest elevators in the world. Three, entourage."

"Why would a fast elevator ruin romance?"

"We can pretend we are alone in one, even if we know security is watching. We just hug, so a slow elevator is nice."

"At least you get to see him. Are you going to keep up the long-distance thing?"

Anne hugged her towel to her. "Yes."

Pounding and shouting interrupted Tate's dream just before he kissed Anne. His mind protested. Not fair! Not even a moment alone in his dreams. Tate sat up just as uniformed police burst into his room.

One grabbed Tate's phone off the charging cord and handed it to a well-dressed man.

"Gilman Tate, are you aware that satellite phones are illegal in China?"

"Of course. That is why I don't have one." Tate got out of bed, his Captain America lounge pants making a statement.

"Nevertheless, every night you make untraceable calls to USA. You are breaking the law."

Tate reached for a T-shirt, the policeman nearest him flinching. Tate held up his hands as a sign of surrender. "Just a shirt."

"Put a shirt on and come out with others."

Mitch and Jared knelt on the floor, hands up. It looked like they had both gotten in a few swings before they were subdued or chose to give up. An officer came in with Debi dressed in her exercise clothes, her hands cuffed behind her back. The officer spoke to his superior in Chinese. "Woman try to fight too."

They let Debi sit on a chair.

"Open your phone." The man thrust Tate's phone at him. Policemen came into the room with laptops, phones, and a tablet, all belonging to the Americans.

Tate looked at Jared and Mitch. Mitch gave him a long, slow blink. Tate opened the main part of the phone with his fingerprint. The app they were looking for required a retinal scan. Tate handed the phone back. The man handed the phone to another in plain clothes.

"He is right. It is not a satellite phone," the second man said in Mandarin.

"Check the others and search the rooms," barked the one in charge in his native language. "Gilman Tate, we will find the illegal phone, and you will be expelled from China and the contract you signed revoked."

The sound of drawers banging and closets being ransacked filled the suite. Tate tried to make eye contact with Mitch or Jared, but whenever either man looked up, his head was pushed back down.

A uniformed officer returned from one of the rooms indicating that he could not bypass the hotel safe to which he had an override key.

"Who is in that room?" The man in charge pointed at Mitch's room.

"Me."

"Why does the safe not open?"

Mitch shrugged.

"Go open it." The man pointed to four officers. "You watch him."

An officer returned from the room across the hall with Debi's passport and money belt and reported that there were no other items of interest. "Just an American blonde but may not be lover like you thought." The officers also didn't realize that all four of them were fluent in Chinese.

Debi's lips twitched the slightest bit. The fact that they'd under estimated Debi's capabilities might be in her favor later. Tate doubted they would arrest them. China didn't need the bad publicity.

Mitch returned with his captors, who were obviously angry that the safe wouldn't open. Knowing Mitch, there wasn't even anything in the safe, as he always counseled his clients to never trust a hotel safe.

Tate's stomach rumbled, unhappy that it hadn't been fed when Tate had been awake for more than an hour. "May I go to the bathroom?" After much discussion, the officers decided the Americans could each have a turn but that they must be supervised. Debi asked for a female officer, who was provided nearly fifteen minutes after the rest of them had taken a turn. Tate wished he'd learned Morse code rather than Farsi. At least then they could blink at each other to communicate.

Tate's phone buzzed. The man in charge looked at the screen. "This is a call from government offices. Why?"

"Not sure. What time is it?"

"Nine thirty." They had been under scrutiny for three hours. No wonder Tate was hungry enough to eat stinky tofu.

"Then I am late to meet with Li Jun. He had papers for me to sign regarding taxes or something."

The man's face grew red, and he used several expletives, not all of them familiar to Tate. "Why did you not say you have a meeting?"

"I don't remember you asking what my schedule was or telling me how long your search would last. I had no idea I might be late."

The man stormed out of the suite with Tate's phone. He returned several minutes later. "Li Jun will come here and bring papers. You will get dressed." Several uniformed officers were assigned to guard them.

Tate's bedroom was in complete disarray. The mattress stood upended, and all his drawers lay open. The pockets of his pants had been turned inside out. Two solemn-faced policemen were tracking his every move. Tate skipped taking a shower and pulled on a pair of jeans and a button-down. No point dressing up for a meeting that could end up with him stuck in a suit the rest of the day.

When Tate returned to the main room, he found the others similarly dressed. The policemen's guns had been put away.

"I will remind you, my officers still armed. You will not make any trouble while Li Jun is here."

A few minutes later, Li Jun arrived with several other well-dressed men. Immediately the man who had been in charge all morning and Li Jun fell into a heated argument. Li Jun stopped the man. "You realize Gilman Tate and all his employees speak excellent Mandarin as well as Cantonese?"

Li Jun turned to Tate. "My deepest apologies for your inconvenience this morning. If you will excuse us, we will find a solution to this matter. Except for the electronics on this table, you are free to pack your belongings." He turned to the man in plain clothes. "Inspector Woo, your officers need only protect the electronics. Gilman Tate will not cause any problems. And he and his friends will not talk." The last part came out as an order.

Tate, Mitch, Jared, and Debi shared a look before heading to their respective rooms. Tate zipped up the lining to his suitcase. The fruitless search had been as thorough as it was destructive. There was no point in packing the remains of his toothpaste. Tate used the last of it to brush his teeth. His electric razor didn't work, and the case felt loose. Tate dumped it in the trash. Maybe Anne would like the five-o'clock shadow. Anne! She should be at work, but if she'd tried to text or call him…She hadn't ever done that during the day. And with the time difference, she shouldn't be calling her parents. He needed to get her phone disabled.

Tate folded his last T-shirt. One of his socks was missing, but that was all as far as he could tell. He assumed his money, credit cards, and passport were with the electronics, where he had last seen them.

Jared sat at one end of the couch, Mitch in one of the chairs. Their suitcases were lined up in front of the TV. Debi entered the room, one of the officers wheeling her bag in. She frowned. "They ruined my favorite curling iron. First no nap, now straight hair."

"No talk!" The officer nearest her pointed to the couch. Tate watched Mitch for a reaction to Debi's comment. *Nap* was a code word the bodyguards used, but Tate wasn't sure of the significance. Whatever it was, it didn't make Mitch happier.

Li Jun returned to the room. "Inspector Woo has played an interesting tape for me, Gilman Tate. You are having a conversation about meeting someone at Shanghai Tower. The problem is there is no outgoing call, and we only hear your conversation, not the other side. This is only possible if you were using a satellite phone like you do when you call the States—an infraction we have ignored. But Woo is convinced it could be a terrorist-attack cleverly disguised as talk with girlfriend. It is well known in all the world you have no girlfriend. He has taken precaution of making sure Shanghai police know and are extra vigilant tonight. We will escort you to airport and put you on first available Chinese plane to USA."

Tate pointed to the four phones, three tablets, and laptop on the table, along with the wallets and passports. "When do we get these back?"

"When you are safely out of country. Also, no entrance without permission for three months. Then, only for you Gilman Tate. Not these employees. They may come back in one year if no problems."

One of the officers scooped all the electronics into a box.

Tate read over the papers Li Jun had brought. "This tax is 1 percent higher than my agreement with Wong International."

"It is a convenience fee. If you wish to not pay, you may stay longer."

So Li Jun had found a way to get a bribe in. Tate signed the form. "Shall we go?"

They were escorted out of the building and into waiting police cars.

18

The line for the Shanghai Tower was longer than they expected. "Should we buy tickets for Tate and his friends?" Anne counted out the yuan for her ticket.

"No, you can wait up there for him. So much more romantic than waiting down here. Once we get up there, you can text him." Sophia took a place in a line that snaked back and forth. Ahead of them, a Caucasian couple pushed a stroller. The line turned again.

"I still don't see them." Anne stood on her tiptoes to see over the crowd.

"Maybe he has a VIP entrance."

"Then he should have shared it with us." Anne followed the line downstairs to the basement level.

"I thought we were going to the top."

"You know the saying—what goes up must come down. Perhaps this is the opposite." They entered the elevator along with a couple dozen of their new, closest friends. A digital screen indicated the speed of the elevator in miles per second. Anne's stomach took a couple floors to catch up with the rest of her body.

No one awaited them as they exited. So much for a VIP entrance. Anne and Sophia circled the observation deck, passing tourists from many countries, based on the different languages the two women heard.

One of the security officers started to follow them. Sophia pointed at one of the windows and pulled out her phone. The officer watched for a moment and returned to his post. Sophia took another photo. "I guess they aren't used to people looking for love up here."

Anne pulled out her phone and took a picture of the river view. They followed the crowd around, taking photos of the scenery and a couple selfies. Anne checked her watch. Tate was forty-five minutes late. She pulled out her Tate phone. It was dead. "I know I charged it last night." She tried turning it off and on. The screen flashed white, then turned black again. "Weird. Have you ever seen a phone do this?"

Sophia took it from her and tried to turn it on but with the same result. "Odd, restarting is usually the first thing IT people tell you to do. You didn't take it in the shower last night, did you?"

"No, it was working this morning. I was going to text Tate, but the oatmeal boiled over." The postage-stamp-sized stove only accommodated play-sized pots and pans, which meant that even diverting your attention for a second could be disastrous when cooking for two.

"I prefer those egg pancakes at the corner vendor anyway. That is one thing I want to learn to make." Sophia handed the phone back. "Did he try to reach you through your regular one?"

"I have no notifications." Anne checked the screen again. "The last one is still that photo my brother sent me of the lake."

Thirty minutes later, they'd completed another circuit of the observation deck. The guard followed them again.

"I think we have worn out our welcome." Sophia pointed to a boat below.

"He is an hour and a half late. This is ending more like Cary Grant than Tom Hanks."

"I don't think we can stay up here long enough to find out which movie this is. Check your chat app again." Sophia took a photo of some random building.

Anne checked the app twice. "I've been ghosted." Anne needed to sit down. It couldn't be true. She checked a third time. Bertram didn't appear anywhere on her contact list. His name didn't even come up when she searched for him.

"No way." Sophia grabbed Anne's phone. "Bertram, right?" Sophia scrolled up and down the list. "You should have hours of chat history."

"I know. It's gone." Anne headed for the elevator. One more minute up here and she would either faint or lose the dinner she hadn't eaten yet.

The elevator's impressive speed didn't help as her insides tried to defy gravity. Sophia held on to Anne's arm—by way of comfort or to keep her from falling, Anne didn't know, but she didn't care. She just needed the support.

Sophia navigated them to the nearest subway. Anne wasn't sure how they got to a McDonald's.

"Consistently good ice cream. Let's order some." Sophia didn't give Anne a chance to protest before ordering two ice creams and dragging Anne to a booth. "Eat."

It wasn't the same as her favorite double-fudge swirl, but it still felt cool as it slid down her throat, which was hot with unshed tears. "No one has ever ghosted me before. That must be why the other phone doesn't work. He killed it. All I have left is a few photos." Anne pulled out her smartphone.

Sophia covered it with her hand. "Three days. Give yourself three days before you delete a single memory. Preferably three weeks. Don't even open them."

Anne met her eyes. "I don't want to wait."

"I know you don't. But you might delete one you regret. You hiked miles of the wall. Hardly anyone does that. You visited Forbidden City. Not many people see that. Don't erase any photos yet."

"Fine." Anne put her phone back in her purse and took another bite of her ice cream. Soon her bowl was empty, though she'd barely tasted any of it.

Sophia cleared their table. "Now, let's go find some dumplings or noodles. Maybe a kabob. I need more than just sugar."

Anne followed Sophia back out to the street. "Nothing too adventurous."

"Noodles it is."

They didn't have to go far to find a vendor. Sophia stopped at another booth and bought a couple dumplings.

Anne looked around. "There is a surprising lack of chocolate here."

"I read that the Chinese eat an average of one bar per year compared to Americans eating ninety."

"I eat more than ninety."

"Me too. We can go to the supermarket. They are most likely to carry some in the foreign-foods area."

"I can't decide what I want to eat first when I get home, a hamburger or chocolate bar."

Sophia laughed. "I'm going to this little place near my house and having their hot-fudge brownie shake and a hamburger."

"That sounds divine. I am joining you."

"Ready to go back to the apartment? I can take a long shower so you can call your mom."

Anne stopped walking. "How did you know I wanted to talk to her?"

"Because that's what I would do right now."

Anne nodded. "Just don't run out of hot water. I'll want a shower too."

Tate, Mitch, Jared, and Debi entered the airport through a heavy metal door and were escorted down a long hallway to a dingy room not unlike the little meeting room Mitch had found for Tate to apologize to Anne. It had a table and a few chairs. Captain Woo took their passports out of the bag the one officer carried. "I'll return with your tickets."

Jared opened his mouth to say something but was cut off when an officer barked, "No talking."

Debi rolled her eyes and relaxed into her chair. Sometime later—without a phone, watch, or window it was impossible to know how long—Mr. Woo returned with their tickets. "Do any of you require medication?"

All of them shook their heads.

"Good, then check in the bags. Two officers will keep your phones and electronics until you leave China." He directed three officers to remove the bags. "We booked you for the 22:00 flight to LA. You will remain in this room until the flight is boarding. Two of my officers will fly with you to make sure you exit the plane."

Debi brushed her hair over her shoulder. "Do we get to eat? I've eaten nothing all day, and I get ill on planes if I am dehydrated."

Captain Woo frowned. "I will ask for a meal to be delivered." He opened the door and spoke to someone in the hallway. "Fifteen minutes and you will have your food. You must understand this is for your safety. If you were to be caught using a satellite phone, you could end up in far worse places than an extradition suite. Next time you need a sat phone, remember you may buy one here from our network."

A headache pulsed in the back of Tate's head. He tried to focus on things he could fix rather than the fact that Anne was going to get stood up and it would be almost a day before he could contact her. If he could. His only small victory was that his app worked and was technically legal. Neither the development team nor he had figured in the variable of local surveillance being alarmed by one-sided conversations. Tate had assumed that after he paid the increased tax, or bribe, he would have been released. Apparently the phone conversation had alarmed someone more than it should have. Inspector Woo left, leaving his officers in charge.

An officer entered with several bags of food and some bottled water. At this point, Tate fully expected a crust of bread and was delighted to find that the food was better than most airport fare. Debi played with her food, as did Mitch. Tate was halfway through his meal when he realized Debi and Mitch were making sure the meals hadn't been drugged. Jared finished his food, still fully alert. Debi started eating hers. Tate slowed his eating. Only after Debi finished and both Jared and Debi seemed fine did Mitch eat. Tate finished his noodles. Did the team often eat like this?

Twenty minutes later, Debi asked to use the restroom. They gave each of them a turn. Tate was taken to a family-style restroom. Rather than follow him in, the officers waited at the door. Other than two or three employees, he saw no one else. He did, however, find a clock and learned it was 6:30 p.m.

What must Anne think of him?

Three hours later they were escorted aboard an empty plane, bypassing the main gate entrance. The seats in coach were set up in a two-four-two configuration. Tate, Jared, Debi, and Mitch were assigned the four seats in the center of the second-to-last row. The officers took the two seats on either side. The rest of the flight boarded.

Tate turned to the nearest officer. "May I have my phone back?"

"Still in China. No phone."

Tate switched to Mandarin. "So, when we are in the air, may I have my phone back?"

"This airplane is Chinese until it lands in LA. You are in China."

Tate stifled a groan. He'd spent most of the last couple hours composing a message to Anne, hoping he remembered enough of the old Cary Grant movie his grandmother liked that Anne might understand his cryptic message. "Had a Ms. Karr moment. Find happiness like Cary did in Hollywood." There was more Tate wanted to explain. He wanted to warn her to destroy the phone. But he knew he would have to use the official app and that every word would be scrutinized. The message was probably too cryptic anyway. The huge leap from Cary Grant finding happiness because he never gave up to returning to the USA by mentioning Hollywood was vague. But the message that he was unavoidably detained might get through.

Mitch shifted in one of the middle seats. No way could the large man be even semicomfortable in a coach seat for the next fifteen hours. The only advantage was that they sat close enough to communicate. Tate leaned over to say something, but Mitch shook his head and pointed to one of the in-flight security cameras directly overhead. Rats. Tate had forgotten about the onboard cameras. He turned on the personal entertainment system in front of him but soon realized his earbuds where in one of the checked bags. One glance at the nearest officer and all thoughts of asking for a pair fled. Did the flight attendants pass them out in coach, or would he need to buy a pair? It had only been four years since Tate had last flown coach, but he couldn't remember that detail, and trans-Pacific flights were bound to be different.

Tate leaned back and waited for the safety announcement. Just fifteen more hours and this day would get better. He would land two hours before he'd departed local time and still have hours left of this Friday to make things better. The joys of flying across the international date line.

Anne would live through most of tomorrow thinking he didn't care.

Anne rubbed the mirror. It didn't help. Her eyes still were puffy and red rimmed. Her first free day in Shanghai, and instead of going on the tour Sophia had arranged, Anne wanted to crawl back into bed. The special cell phone Tate had given her refused to work after charging all night, and no matter what she typed in, she couldn't find Tate or Debi on the Chinese chat app. It wasn't her first breakup, but she'd seen those coming. It was her first time being ghosted. She'd thought the coworker who'd cut her ex-boyfriend off by ghosting him last winter cruel. The boyfriend hadn't been a stalker or abusive. He deserved better than such a harsh breakup.

Fine. She didn't need him. Anne marched back into the bedroom—well, the only room since it was also the kitchen—and picked up the phone Tate had given her. She wrenched off the back, removed the sim card, and snapped it in half. Then she returned to the bathroom and flushed the little card down the toilet. There was probably some law against foreign objects in Chinese toilets since they didn't even flush toilet paper, but she didn't care.

"What are you doing?"

"Don't worry. I'm not getting rid of photos. There weren't any on this phone. But he gave it to me, and I wanted—" Anne slumped onto the lower bunk, currently converted back into the futon couch, in tears.

Sophia sat next to her and wrapped an arm around Anne's shoulders. "Maybe there is another explanation."

"Yes, aliens were interested in his language-learning software and beamed him up. Hundreds probably saw a giant UFO, but a government conspiracy keeps it off the news." Anne hiccup laughed though her tears.

"That would be an explanation. I can just imagine Mitch and Jared taking on laser ray guns."

"Sorry I'm such a mess."

"Get dressed. We don't want to miss our water-village day trip. Besides, it will give you a reason not to talk if your mom calls again to check on you since you never returned her call." Sophia gathered her clothes and entered the tiny bathroom.

Anne wiped her eyes again. They had paid more than usual for the tour of the water villages. Sophia was right. Anne would regret missing it. She'd only been dating Tate for a week. It felt longer, but all evidence of their texts and conversations had disappeared. At least she didn't have to reread them. She pulled out her Bradford alumni T-shirt, soft from wear, and put it on with some denim shorts. She wished she'd brought her dorm T-shirt. Even though she hadn't done anything crown-worthy yet, she loved thinking she could be Miscellaneous Royalty. Just as long as she didn't get a crown for Miss Led. So what if her heart had lied to her?

Sophia emerged from the bathroom. "Let's go."

Anne grabbed her purse and followed her friend out.

An hour before they were to land, one of the flight attendants asked an officer to take a call in the galley. The officer returned a few minutes later and opened his overhead bin, then took out the bag containing the phones, tablets, and computer and handed it to Tate. "Humblest and most sincere apologies. Inspector Woo was too hasty. He no longer holds office. You were mistakenly held. Chinese government most anxious to make things right. May take a few weeks to reinstate visas." The officer bowed and sat back down.

Jared took the bag and distributed the phones, passports, and other contents of the bag. He kept his head down as he spoke. "So, this goes under the 'all this was a big mistake' category?"

Debi counted her money. "I think they made us pay for our own dinner."

Mitch laughed. "I wonder if Tate's credit card paid for our last-minute flights."

Tate scrolled through his phone, hoping to be able to connect to the plane's Wi-Fi and send a message. "Is anyone else's Chinese chat app missing?"

"My special Tate game app is disabled too." Jared held up his phone.

Mitch smiled. "That just means Seattle did their job."

Aware they were still being monitored, Tate refrained from asking how anyone in Seattle had learned there was a problem and triggered the fail-safe, remotely disabling the apps and Anne's phone. He'd never warned her that her phone would self-corrupt if something happened and they pulled the software quickly. Without the text app and her phone disabled, Tate had no way to contact her.

Her parents. They knew how to contact her.

Now if he could figure out how to contact them. Right after he landed. No way was he going to trust the Chinese Wi-Fi. Maybe he shouldn't trust his contract, either.

"Admit it. This is so much better than our apartment." Sophia raised her phone to take another photo.

"You are right. I am thinking about going back to that shop and buying one of the traditional dresses. Even though I've come to realize many things about my DNA versus where I belong, it would still be cool to have something like what Great-grandma might have worn."

"I think the ones we tried on were just for photos, like the Old West family photos you take at amusement parks. We'll have to ask the teachers where you can buy a quality dress that won't use all your summer savings."

"How many SD cards worth of photos have you gone through?"

"Oh, I have been deleting as I go." Sophia swung around and snapped a photo of Anne.

"Don't do that. I look horrid today."

"Actually, your eyes aren't puffy anymore."

"Don't! I am trying not to go there. I've handled breakups before. I can do this one." Anne looked out over the canal that ran between the buildings. This area was so calm compared to the big cities she had been in. Shanghai even made Boston seem small.

"Hey, look at that little dog," Sophia said, changing the subject. The dog must have been her first idea.

"I think that is the first dog I've seen in a while."

Anne and Sophia continued their tour. Anne was determined to wait until she was in the privacy of the shower that night to let the tears fall again.

Tate worked out the time difference in his head. They'd landed at 7:00 p.m. Friday night in LA after taking off at ten-ish Friday night in Beijing. So, for Anne, it was lunchtime on Saturday. He needed to work fast.

As soon as they cleared customs, Mitch found them a quiet corner. "What is our plan?"

"My plan is to safely contact Anne. She must think I hate her."

"How are you going to do that?" asked Jared.

"With our app off-line, her second phone is useless, and none of us can get back on the Chinese chat, which I don't trust anyway. Someone needs to contact her in person."

"As your head of security, I don't approve of you returning to China." Mitch crossed his arms in a classic bodyguard don't-mess-with-me stance.

"What about Hong Kong? Different rules. I can be in Hong Kong without a visa for ninety days if it isn't business."

"How do you get her to Hong Kong?" asked Debi.

"I get her parents to bring her there."

Jared shook his head. "She will not up and leave her job to go to Hong Kong."

"I know, but the other teacher could go back, the one who wasn't sick. Then she will be jobless again."

"You can't know that." Debi shook her head.

"Guys, work with me. If I get a red-eye to Boston, I can be at her parents' by morning. If I can talk them into helping me, I can have them on a flight by Saturday afternoon, and they will get to Shanghai Sunday night. If they talk her into it, she could get on a flight Sunday night and be in Hong Kong by midnight Sunday. If Sophia will cover for her, she can be back at the school by 11:00 a.m. Monday—earlier if I can talk one of my HK acquaintances with their own plane into helping with the Hong Kong-to-Shanghai section. She might not miss any work."

Jared looked from Mitch to Debi and back. "Let's get a private jet to Boston. We all need sleep, and Mitch doesn't have anyone else on his team who speaks Chinese. It also gives us time to catch our lawyers up on what just happened and decide what we want to do about the contract you just signed."

"I don't care how much money we lose. I think I made a huge mistake. But I don't care about that now."

Debi looked up from her phone. "I can get us a Learjet in three hours. That gives us time to run to a hotel to shower and change, etc. I don't care if it is still Friday on my phone, my last shower Thursday morning was like sixty hours ago."

Tate pulled out his private credit card. "Do whatever it takes. Money is no object—I so love saying that sometimes."

Debi made a few calls to arrange for transportation while Mitch checked in with his security team in Seattle. Jared called the lawyers. Tate did an internet search to find the Williams's address in Shrewsbury, Massachusetts. Amazing how knowing the town could narrow it down to the right Williams family.

Debi got off the phone and waved for everyone to follow her. "Hotel shuttle will come get us in five. The suites were full, so I got us two sets of adjoining rooms across the hall from each other. I also added new electric razors and a curling wand from the hotel shop to the bill. They should be in our rooms, and room service will deliver hamburgers to everyone in forty-five minutes."

"Debi, I am sure I don't pay you enough. If anyone needs anything, just charge it to the room."

Mitch stopped them. "I'm going to go back to Seattle tonight, then I'll turn around in the morning for Hong Kong. If you want to pare down your luggage, I'll take the extra bags back. My flight leaves in two and a half hours."

"Thanks. I wasn't looking forward to running around with my dirty clothes." Debi grinned.

Jared slapped Tate on the shoulder. "Be prepared for that bill from the hotel gift shop. I think Debi just bought a new wardrobe."

"If that is what it takes." Tate smiled. This could work.

"I don't know. I've never been ghosted before!" Anne choked back tears during the video call.

"What exactly is 'ghosted?'" asked her father.

Her sister, Emilee, answered him. "It's where you dump a significant other by cutting them off. Block calls, texts, erase them from your social media, everything, and turn them into a ghost. Only he hadn't put her on social media, so her friends don't know she has been ghosted. That is the worst—when your mutual friends know."

"And you are sure this is what he did, Anne?" asked Mom.

"My only other theory is that Martians heard about it and kidnapped him."

"Uh-huh, abducted by aliens. Way to go, sis." Gareth brought a smile to her face.

"Anyway, not talking about him anymore. Today Sophia and I went and saw the water village, like Venice, only in China. Way cool."

"What are you doing tomorrow?" asked Mom in keeping with the change of subject.

"Mostly shopping. I want a traditional dress—if I can get one for less than two thousand yuan or $300. I didn't find myself or my heritage here. I'm American, and I belong with our crazy, multiflavored family. But it would be cool to own something like my great-grandmother could have worn, at least to wear on school culture days."

"So, you are satisfied with your trip?" asked her other sister, Katelyn.

"Yes, I've had China on my bucket list forever. I thought I was missing something. But this isn't my land. I missed fried chicken on the Fourth of July, although KFC is huge over here and we did go there, it wasn't the same. And in case I haven't said it enough, I love all of you. And thank you, Mom and Dad, for adopting me."

Mom fanned her face. "Don't you dare make me cry, Anne love."

Anne covered a yawn. "I need to go to bed, and you need to start whatever Saturday project you have. Night! Or good morning, family. Love you."

Anne disconnected the call and hurried for the shower so she could cry in private.

Tate stood on the front porch of the two-story colonial. Inside, a dog barked and someone shouted at it to be quiet. A man about Tate's age and of African descent opened the door. "What are you doing here? You leave my sister crying and have the nerve to show up here?"

A man in his fifties came down the stairs. "Gareth, what is going on?"

"Tate Gilman is getting off our porch and leaving before I make him leave."

Tate was glad he'd left Jared and Debi in the rented SUV. He doubted Gareth would take a swing at him, but he didn't need the bodyguards in the middle of this. "Please, if you'll give me a moment to explain. I need your help."

Mr. Williams tapped his son's shoulder. "Go find your mom. I'm sure whatever brought Mr. Gilman to our front door is important. Come on in and have a seat." Mr. Williams leaned out the front door. "Are those your bodyguards? They are welcome to come inside. They'll melt in our July heat."

Tate shook his head. "They have the AC running, and we've all decided that if someone is to take a swing at me, they won't interfere because time is of the essence and I only want a chance to explain."

Mr. Williams held out his arm, indicating for Tate to go into the living room. Mrs. Williams and two women Tate recognized from Anne's photos as her sisters followed her into the room. "This is my family. As you can see, everyone, other than Anne, made it home for the holiday."

Tate swallowed. When he'd planned this, he only envisioned speaking to Anne's parents. "As you know, I'm Tate and I love Anne—"

"Then why did you ghost her?" Gareth stepped forward from the wall he'd been leaning against.

"I didn't ghost her."

One sister snorted.

"Friday morning just before seven, several members of a Chinese police department showed up at my hotel. They deprived my team of all electronics and escorted us from the country. I had no way to contact Anne. When my bodyguards did not check in, the tech team in Seattle took several security measures, including disabling a phone I gave Anne so she could contact me. When we got our phones back, we discovered the Chinese government had disabled access to the chat app. Our visas have also been revoked. I can't reach Anne. I need your help."

Mrs. Williams pulled out her phone.

"Stop. Don't use your phone. I don't want Anne in danger. I am 99 percent sure everything on their chat app is monitored. They watch for keywords. Even though I have received a kind of apology, nothing formal, I am not sure they aren't looking for the person in Shanghai they believe I called with an 'illegal satellite phone.'"

"Then what do you need us to do?" asked Mr. Williams.

"I came here to ask if the two of you will fly to Shanghai. I have a hold on two business-class tickets for this afternoon's flight. You'll be there by Sunday evening Shanghai time. Convince Anne to go to Hong Kong with you. I can meet her there and explain what happened. One of my acquaintances who lives in Hong Kong will provide his private plane for the trip, and Anne can be back in time for work on Monday."

Mrs. Williams spoke first. "My passport expired. I renewed it, but it hasn't arrived yet."

"I never got around to renewing mine." Mr. Williams shook his head.

"When will we get back?" asked Katelyn.

"It depends. You can stay in Shanghai up to 144 hours. I'll pay for your hotel. The earliest you could come back is Monday around noon, Shanghai time, which would put you back in the US on Monday around noon.

Katelyn shook her head. "Sorry, I am due in court at 11:00 a.m. Monday.

Gareth uncrossed his arms and stepped forward. "What do you intend to tell my sister if she goes to Hong Kong?"

Tate looked Gareth in the eye, then looked at Anne's parents. "The truth—that I love her smile and her jokes and the way she gets lost when she has directions but can't follow a map. Her sense of honor. Did you know she got sacked from her job in Xi'an because she basically refused to bribe me into funding an orphanage? She didn't even tell me that was the reason. Look, I know it is fast. We've mostly been texting this past month, and I don't know that she is ready for me to ask for her hand, but as soon as she is, I hope I have your blessing—as well as hers."

"She still has five or six weeks in China. How are you going to keep the relationship going if you are banned from the country?"

"Email mostly. Hong Kong when she can."

Anne's mother raised her eyebrows.

"In separate hotel rooms, of course. Sophia can come too." Tate amended his statement.

"I wish I could go, but my rotation in pediatrics starts tomorrow," said Emilee.

Gareth had gone back to leaning against the wall, arms crossed. There was no backup plan.

"I have another week off. My passport is at my apartment in Boston. I'll go, but know this: you make her cry again, and I'll punch you out like I wanted to when we were in the seventh grade." Gareth pushed off the wall with his shoulder and extended his hand. "Besides, who would think an African native is connected to the two of you? I'll just be a random tourist."

Tate shook Gareth's hand. "If I make her cry again, you may have to get in line behind at least one of my bodyguards."

Gareth turned to his parents. "I'll let you know how things go." He hugged them and his sisters.

Tate went to shake Mr. Williams's hand and was pulled into a hug. "I hope this works. I'd be proud to call you son."

Mrs. Williams also hugged him. "Find a way to contact her more. I know she is hiding behind that cyber wall, but find a way."

"I will, Mrs. Williams. I will."

"Call me Julies."

"Yes, ma'am."

Gareth bounded back down the stairs, carry-on in hand. "Let's do this."

Tate turned to the rest of the family. "For Anne's safety, please don't mention me by name. And don't let her know what is going on. You never know who is listening." He followed Gareth out to the SUV. In less than twenty-four hours, he could talk to Anne.

Hey, sis, whatcha doing? Anne read her brother's text.

Shopping. Or I was. I am eating black-coconut ice cream right now. What has you up so early? I thought you slept in on Sundays.

— **Just chilin'. Is Sophia with you?**

Yes.

—**Do you have your passports?**

Of course.

—**Then I need you two to come to the Shanghai airport. I'll text you the terminal as soon as I figure it out.**

Anne showed Sophia her screen. "What do you think is going on?"

"With your brother? Nothing predictable. Maybe he was bored and hopped a flight to come visit you.

—**Are you at the airport?**

Waiting to get through customs.

"My brother is insane!"

Sophia stuffed the last of her black ice cream cone into her mouth and nodded. She swallowed before speaking. "Our apartment is on the way. Let's drop our packages off. We can be at the airport in forty minutes."

We can be to the airport in about forty min.

—**See you soon.**

Anne ate the rest of her cone as fast as she could. "Ouch! Brain freeze."

"Let's go." Sophia navigated them to the apartment and then to the mag rail. As she'd predicted, forty-two minutes later, they arrived at the airport.

Gareth waited just outside the exit to the platform. He engulfed Anne in a hug. "I've missed you." He nodded at Sophia. "Hey."

"You are crazy. What are you doing here?" Sophia had her hand on her hip.

"A brother knows when his sister needs support. Besides, I am always up for an adventure. So here I am. Now, if you ladies will come this way, I have a car waiting."

"Car? We don't need a car. The mag train is right here." Anne pointed behind them.

"Have I ever steered you wrong?"

"I don't think you want your sister to answer that."

Gareth shook his head. "Fine, when it's really mattered, have I ever let you down?"

"No."

"Good, then trust me just for an hour or so." Gareth held out his hands, palms up. Anne took one hand, Sophia the other. He escorted them to a black limo.

"Gareth?"

"One hour, sis."

The limo didn't follow the exit signs. Anne tensed. Perhaps she'd misread them. They stopped at a smaller terminal.

"What is going on?" Sophia eyed Gareth suspiciously.

"We are taking a private jet to Hong Kong. Don't worry. You'll be back before breakfast." Gareth exited the car.

Sophia's mouth hung open. "Don't worry?" she mouthed to Anne.

Anne shrugged. "I told him I'd give him an hour."

A man with a sign reading "Gareth" waited for them. "This way, please."

Compared to the main airport, security here was minimal.

They boarded the plane out on the tarmac. Anne ran her hand over the supple leather seats. "Gareth? How did you get this plane?"

Gareth checked his watch. "Half hour more of trust, please."

They buckled themselves into their seats. The man who met them at the limo pointed out the safety features, then entered the cockpit.

Takeoff was smooth, and soon the lights of Shanghai were behind them.

Anne checked her phone. "Your hour is up. Spill."

Gareth grinned, his teeth flashing white against his dark skin. "It all started yesterday morning about a half hour after our family phone call when you bravely didn't cry."

Anne glared at her brother. "Don't go there."

"Fine, I'll skip over that. Someone knocked at the door, and that drove the dog crazy. So I opened the door, and it was this man. I knew the moment I saw him he wanted to sell me something."

"A salesman?" Sophia crossed her arms and narrowed her eyes.

"Let me finish. This man had a story. It was very compelling—so compelling I decided to help him solve a problem he has with the Chinese government."

Anne closed her eyes in exasperation. "You're not making sense."

"See, that is part of my problem. I can't tell you his story. He must do that. But you need to know that I believed what he told me or I wouldn't be here. Now, just relax. Once we are in Hong Kong, I can explain the rest."

Sophia leaned forward. "Should I ask them to turn the plane around?"

Anne studied her brother. "Mom and Dad didn't rescue you early enough. You learned too much about practical jokes in Madagascar. But I warn you—payback will be double, so help me, if we get fired over this little stunt. You'll pay the company whatever we both owe them." Anne sat back in her seat. This had something to do with Tate. She was sure of it. At the moment, the abducted-by-aliens scenario looked pretty good.

Tate paced the luxury condo his friend had loaned him. Debi glared at him. "That will not get her here any faster."

"Why can't I go to the airport?"

"Low-key, remember? The less you are seen, the better this will go. Mitch still isn't overly comfortable with you being here." Debi's phone buzzed. "You can officially stop pacing. The car just pulled up in front."

Tate stared at the private elevator, willing it to open. Finally, the ping sounded as the elevator reached his floor. The doors opened. Gareth stood behind Anne, his hands over her eyes. Sophia sucked in a loud breath and clamped her hands over her mouth. Gareth urged his sister forward.

Tate stood with his arms wide as Gareth removed his hands.

"Tate?" Anne didn't rush into his arms as he hoped, and he dropped them to his side.

"I had a small snafu with a government official. He took our phones, and we got kicked out of the country."

Anne took a curious step forward. "Then why did you ghost me?"

"I didn't. Part of it was a safety protocol, and part was me being blocked from the chat app. As soon as I got to the US, I went to your parents."

"You talked to my parents?" She took another step forward.

Tate nodded. "And your sisters and Gareth. I needed help contacting you before the government accused you of breaking laws."

Anne looked over her shoulder to where her brother stood. "You convinced him to come help you, and he didn't punch you first?"

Tate opened his arms and took a step toward Anne. "I can be very convincing when I want to be."

Anne closed the distance and wrapped her arms around his waist. "I can't believe you are here and you talked to my parents. What did you say to get Gareth to come?"

"I told them the truth—that I love you." Tate lifted Anne's chin, not bothering to see if his audience had taken the hint and left the room.

Anne's hands slid up his chest. "I love you too." Then she pulled him down to meet her in a kiss.

Epilogue

Anne checked her reflection in the mirror. The jade Chinese silk dress was ready for tonight, and she was too. It was the annual fundraiser for the children's hospital. Everyone on Seattle's who's-who list would be at the event, along with celebrity watchers and paparazzi. She'd made Tate and Debi walk her through the protocols a dozen times. Since she'd returned from China in mid-August, Debi and Mitch had done everything they could to let her and Tate have as normal a dating life as possible. With the help of her mother, Anne found a job at a private elementary and moved to Seattle within a week of returning to the States. She'd had enough of long-distance relationships to last a lifetime.

The fact that for most of her last weeks in China, communications had been reduced to emails through her brother's or sisters' accounts, which limited romantic exchanges completely, played a huge role in the decision to trade coasts to be closer to Tate. The two weekends they managed to meet in Hong Kong, they'd talked almost nonstop to catch up. She'd contemplated forfeiting her contract and skipping out on the immersion camp portion of the summer, but Tate and Sophia convinced her to finish the stay. They'd been correct, Anne had no regrets and spoke passable Chinese thanks to some of the college students.

Someone tapped on her door. "Miss Williams, Mr. Gilman is here." Another thing to get used to. Margo, the unassuming forty-something housekeeper, doubled as a bodyguard and was just as deadly as Debi. Tate insisted Anne have a safety net in place before they went public.

Anne opened the door.

Margo smiled. "You look beautiful. If he doesn't tell you that, you let me know. Debi taught me a new move I want to try out." Margo stayed upstairs.

Tate waited in the center of her little foyer. Love with a hint of desire filled his eyes. He bent down and kissed her. "You look amazing. Are you ready?"

Anne nodded, and he escorted her to the waiting limo.

"I hope you don't mind, but we have a quick stop to make."

Anne took Tate's hand. "Are you delaying the inevitable when I trip over my feet and exit the photo area through the entrance?"

"That won't happen."

"How do you know?"

"Because I'll be holding on to you the entire time." Tate kissed her nose.

The limo stopped in an empty parking lot. "Where are we? Are we lost?"

"Never."

They exited the car, and Tate took the sidewalk to a building reminiscent of many of the pagodas Anne had seen in China. "What is this place?"

"Seattle's Chinese Garden. Normally closed now, but I convinced them to let me in." Tate led her to the center of the courtyard.

Anne looked around in wonder as the sunset cast a warm glow over the flowers and the building.

Tate went to one knee. Anne tried to listen to the words he was saying—something about being amazing, beautiful, and his future. She nodded before he got to the relevant question and presented a ring.

"A thousand times, yes. Wǒ ài nǐ!" Anne wrapped her arms around him before he could stand, then kissed him just in case he hadn't understood her Chinese answer.

Tate laughed as she pulled back. "So I take it you don't want a long engagement?"

"No. I know where I am going, and I don't want to take any detours."

Tate slipped the ring on her finger and kissed her again. "I think I can accommodate that wish. I have one more thing for you." He opened his wallet, pulled out a folded notebook paper, and handed it to Anne.

Anne turned it over.

"I wrote that a few days after I gave you the other note."

Anne unfolded it.

> Dear Anne,
>
> Will you marry me?
>
> Yes or no?
>
> Bertram

Anne covered her mouth and laughed. "Do you have a pen?"

Misadventures in Love Website

Some of you may have seen the photos of our own Anne Williams last week in her stunning silk dress. After years of entering the wrong classroom and getting lost on her way to practically everywhere, Anne has found her way into the heart of one of the country's newest billionaires. According to my source, they kindled the romance in China, where Anne was fulfilling a bucket-list wish to visit the land of her birth. I hereby crown her Miss Oriented and wish the soon-to-be-wed alumnus many happy returns.

PS. The thrilled groom has donated a year's supply of roses to be sent to crown recipients.

acknowledgments

This story started with my daughter's desire to go to China. Ironically I wrote several of Anne and Tate's tourist scenes in this book the same day my daughter was half a world away visiting the same places. I drew many stories from my sister-in-law's experiences teaching English in China. Thanks Debbie.

Huge thanks to my beta readers and proofreaders, especially Tammy and Nanette for their willingness to read things so many times. I would never make it through a day without Sally whose advice keeps me going.

Thanks also to Michele at Eschler Editing for the edits and finding oh so many little things to fix; any mistakes left in this book are not her fault. Nor are my excellent proofreaders to be blamed. Thank you ladies and gents!

My family, for sharing their home with the fictional characters who often got fed better than they did. And my husband who encouraged me every crazy step of the way, and who is my example for every love story I dream up. The real one is better.

And to my Father in Heaven for putting these wonderful people, and any I may have forgotten to mention, in my life. I am grateful for every experience and blessing I have been granted.

about the author

Lorin Grace was born in Colorado and has moved around the country ever since, living in eight states and several imaginary worlds. She graduated from Brigham Young University with a degree in Graphic Design.

Currently, she lives in northern Utah with her husband, four children, and a dog who is insanely jealous of her laptop. When not writing Lorin enjoys creating graphics, visiting historical sites, perusing museums, and reading.

Lorin is an active member of the League of Utah Writers and was awarded Honorable Mention in their 2016 creative writing contest short romance story category. Her debut novel, *Waking Lucy,* was awarded a 2017 Recommended Read award in the LUW Published book contest. In 2018 Mending Fences with the Billionaire, also received a Recommended Read award.

You can learn more about her, and sign up for her writers club at loringrace.com or at Facebook: LorinGraceWriter

www.ingramcontent.com/pod-product-compliance
Lightning Source LLC
Chambersburg PA
CBHW070528260626
47161CB00004B/1656